Secrets...
& Scandal

...Plus!

DO YOU BOTTLE THINGS UP?
TRY OUR FAB QUIZ AT
THE BACK OF THE BOOK

**SOME SECRETS ARE JUST TOO GOOD TO KEEP
TO YOURSELF!**

Sugar
SECRETS...

...& Scandal

Mel Sparke

Collins
An Imprint of HarperCollins*Publishers*

Published in Great Britain by Collins in 2000
Collins is an imprint of HarperCollins*Publishers* Ltd
77–85 Fulham Palace Road, Hammersmith, London W6 8JB

The HarperCollins website address is
www.fireandwater.com

9 8 7 6 5 4 3 2 1

Creative consultant: Karen McCombie
Copyright © Sugar 2000. Licensed with TLC

ISBN 0 00 675431 7

Printed and bound in Great Britain by
Caledonian International Book Manufacturing Ltd, Glasgow

CHAPTER 1

● ●

I SEE A TALL, DARK STRANGER...

"No – I don't want to."

"Oh, come on, Maya!"

"No, Sonja – I don't believe in that kind of thing."

"You don't have to take it seriously, if that's what's bothering you. It's just a bit of fun!" Sonja Harvey whined. Beside her, Kerry Bellamy gave a wide-eyed nod of agreement.

"If Maya feels uncomfortable with this, then she doesn't have to do it," Anna Michaels interrupted, trying to be the voice of reason. Normally, that was Maya's job, but since she was on the receiving end of Sonja's wheedling at that moment, someone had to step in. Anyway, Anna felt responsible.

"Oh, Anna, she's just making a big deal about nothing," snorted Catrina Osgood. "C'mon,

5

Maya, put your camera down for once and stop being so boring and sensible."

Before Maya Joshi could splutter out any more protests, Cat had pulled her friend's camera out of her hands and was propelling her towards a benevolently smiling woman, dressed in a cosy cardie, with a set of tarot cards in front of her.

"We're all in this together," Cat whispered to Maya. "And if *you* don't do it then Kerry'll probably start getting the wobbles and pull out."

Maya glanced round and saw Anna, Kerry and Sonja making their way over to other benevolently smiling women dotted further along the large hall, although with their swirls of tie-dye and swathes of velvet, they seemed more spookily exotic than the psychic in front of Maya.

"But if *you* lot are all getting your futures told, I don't see why you need me to—"

"Don't be a hypocrite," Cat hissed at her. "You can't come along to a Psychic Fair and think you can ask all these people to pose for you if you don't even give them a chance to show you what they can do..."

The pressure on Maya's shoulder was inescapable. Cat was pressing her down into the plastic chair across the table from the woman in the cardie. There was no way out.

"Hello, dear," smiled the tarot-reader. "Let's see what we can do for you today, shall we?"

Maya's world revolved around logic and common sense, not around anything remotely supernatural.

So why's it sending shivers up my spine? she wondered silently.

• • •

"You have a worry on your mind at the moment."

Anna looked at the runes and wondered how these small stones with their ancient pagan markings could spell that out. But it was true: she was worried. Worried that the other girls were going to regret giving up their Sunday to come to this fair in the city. It had been Anna's idea, and now she'd seen what was on offer, she wasn't convinced that it had been a very good idea.

True, her friends seemed genuinely interested in the stalls and demonstrations – with everything from books on *How To Find Your Inner Angel* to aura reading – but Anna knew they were all (apart from Maya) mostly excited about consulting the real-live psychics who could give them a glimpse into their futures.

But I hope the other psychics are doing a better job than this one, fretted Anna, *or the girls will be demanding their entrance fees back from me...*

Much as she was fascinated by all things spiritual, Anna hadn't admitted to the other girls beforehand that she was apprehensive about getting a reading done. There had been too many painful events in her life that might be revealed – the destructive relationship with her ex, the terrible rows with her mother, the baby... No one but her brother Owen knew about any of her past and that's the way Anna wanted it to stay. But would some mind-reading, soul-searching stranger have the ability to expose these old, hidden wounds, she worried?

But she needn't have. So far, the rune-casting woman had told her that she had a warm and loving bond with her mother, a great boyfriend and a job with fabulous prospects. The last one made her laugh the most: much as she was grateful to have come across Nick and his offer of a job with a flat thrown in, being a waitress at the End-of-the-Line café was hardly the start of a high-powered career.

"I think I know what you're worrying about," the woman nodded sagely. "You sense a conflict between your love-life and your career."

"Actually, that's not really something I've been too bothered about," Anna smiled.

Considering I don't have a love-life or a career...

• • •

"Ah, I see that you have Scandinavian blood," mused the henna red-head as she pored over Sonja's palm.

Don't know why she needs to study my hand for that, thought Sonja sceptically. *She just has to look at the rest of me.*

Sonja tossed her honey-blonde hair back and fixed her sky-blue eyes – both attributes inherited from her Swedish mother – on the woman across the table. She became so engrossed in the psychic's ornately beaded, dangly earrings that she wasn't really concentrating on what the woman said next.

"...he has blonde hair too."

"Who has?" Sonja demanded.

"The one you love."

Owen had brown hair. And he was the only one Sonja loved. She was about to tell the woman that she couldn't be more wrong when she caught a glimpse of the earnest look on the not-so-psychic psychic's face. Sonja didn't have the heart to contradict her, so she just smiled non-committally.

"You and he are very close," said the woman, scrutinising the lines in Sonja's hand once again. "The two of you are never apart if you can help it!"

We're never together and we can't help that! Sonja sulked to herself, thinking of Owen sitting in the flat she'd never seen, many long, lonely miles away from her.

"He works with animals."

He's a web designer, Sonja mentally corrected her.

"And I see that you are interested in the field of medicine."

Public relations, actually.

"You're the oldest child in your family..."

I'm the youngest.

"...and the only girl."

What, apart from my two older sisters?

"How does this all sound?"

"Great," Sonja lied. "Worth every penny..."

Shoving her purse back in her pocket, Sonja ambled over to the cafeteria area where the girls had all agreed to meet after they'd been 'done'.

So that's where I've been going wrong, Sonja

laughed to herself. *There I was thinking I was having a long-distance fling with a dark-haired web designer, when I've actually got a blond vet boyfriend. Bet all the little brothers I'm supposed to have just love him...*

• • •

Kerry felt her heart pitter-patter its way through a lambada of palpitations.

The woman in front of her had been silent for what felt like an awfully long time, her electric-blue streaked eyelids eerily closed. A large pink crystal pendant hung around her neck, reflecting the overhead fluorescent lights as her ample chest heaved in and out with concentration.

That's a rose quartz, Kerry noted, her eyes drawn to the crystal.

She'd seen big chunks of the stone earlier, piled up alongside a myriad of other semi-precious stones on stalls round the hall. Kerry also had a tiny fragment of rose quartz in her chakra necklace – a birthday present from Anna last year.

In fact, the necklace – a fine, black leather strip interspersed with tiny pieces of uneven, semi-precious stones – was what Kerry's psychic was holding in her hands, trying to use this favourite possession to tune into the fortunes of the girl who owned it.

"Mmmmmmm..." intoned the psychic suddenly.

Kerry started imperceptibly on her uncomfortable plastic chair.

"There was an event recently..."

She must mean the crash, Kerry thought, her heart thudding. It had been a month since the accident; she'd been in the back of Mr Gladwin's car when his son, Joe, having his first driving lesson, had swerved to avoid a deer on the road. Her broken collarbone and cracked ribs were still giving her niggles of pain, but she didn't let on in front of Joe – he felt guilty enough as it was.

"It was a happy event," the psychic continued.

Not the crash then, obviously, Kerry realised. "Er, well, I'm pretty happy most of the time, but I can't think of one particular event..."

"No one got married? Engaged even?" The woman fixed her with a penetrating look.

"No."

"No one close to you had a baby recently or announced they were pregnant, perhaps?"

Kerry racked her brains and tried to be helpful. Her mum's friend at work had had a baby, but surely that was too distant?

"No," Kerry was forced to respond.

"No matter," said the woman, before taking another deep and meaningful breath.

"I see..." she began again, "that you are a twin."

Kerry flinched; well, that was wrong for a start.

"Um no..." she said warily. "But my boyfriend is a twin."

"Ahhh... that'll be it," nodded the woman, her crystal reflecting the light. "This boyfriend, he is quite a lot older than you...:"

"Um, only about three months older than me actually."

"I meant he is older than you in spirit terms, not in years."

"Oh," replied Kerry, feeling well and truly chastised, if a little confused.

"This boy," said the psychic, closing her eyes again and taking a deep, reflective breath, "he's a very serious young man."

Ollie? Serious? Is she *serious?* thought Kerry, visualising her boyfriend's smiley face and twinkling eyes.

"Well, I wouldn't exactly say he was serious," Kerry tried to explain. "He's always fooling around..."

"Ah, the clowns are always the ones who are crying on the inside," the woman said enigmatically.

"I see," muttered Kerry, although she didn't.

"You must take care of this boy. He and his twin brother—"

"Sister," interrupted Kerry.

"—sister, are very, very close and he worries more for her than for himself."

Kerry opened her mouth and closed it again without saying anything. She thought of Ollie and Natasha's relationship; they weren't particularly close, especially since Tasha'd moved away to London to work. Even back when she was just a pretty girl in Winstead, as opposed to a well-paid model jetting off to various exotic locations, they hadn't been anything other than a typical brother and sister, who fought and teased each other and rubbed along OK.

"I see," repeated Kerry, for want of anything else to say.

"Now this boy has another love apart from you..."

Kerry gulped. OK, so nothing else had been very accurate so far, but maybe the psychic was just warming up. Maybe the amazing – and alarming – insights were just about to start.

"His other love is his hobby, which is... sport, isn't it?"

"Er, music."

"Music – exactly."

Kerry looked expectantly at the big-bosomed woman and waited for more.

"Well, the two of you will be together for ever and be very happy," she finally rattled off brusquely. "Sorry, dear – that's all I'm getting today. It sometimes just works that way."

"Er, thank you," said Kerry dubiously as she fumbled in her purse.

She'd had more insights from the red plastic fortune-telling fish in her cracker on Christmas Day than she'd had here today.

• • •

"What do you see?" demanded Cat, staring mystified at the three old coins she'd just thrown down.

"Interesting..." said the psychic whose card said she specialised in I Ching readings. "I have to consult my book for one moment."

Cat tapped her long, metallic, lavender-painted nails on the table. The tension of waiting to find out the answer to the question she'd just asked made her feel like having a cigarette, but red-ringed No Smoking signs loomed all around her in the bustling hall. And anyway, these days she only ever smoked when her friends weren't around; their narking disapproval always did her head in.

"Ah, now, in answer to your question, your future is to look to the wisdom of others and not just to your own counsel."

"What?" said Cat, crinkling her nose up in confusion. "What does that mean when it's at home?"

"Well, as it says – the wisdom of others in conjunction with your own wisdom will show you the way forward," repeated the black-clad woman.

"But what's that got to do with anything?" blustered Cat. "*Am* I going to be famous or not?"

"Only the wisdom of others can tell you that," intoned the woman with infuriating patience, "as well as your own—"

"—my own wisdom. Yeah, yeah," said Cat sarcastically. "Listen, can we dump that one for a second and try another question?"

"By all means."

The psychic seemed unruffled by Cat's blunt tone and watched serenely as Cat rattled the coins in her hand, ready to ask her question and throw them for an answer.

"Right – will I get married?"

The woman noted the configuration of the fallen coins on a small pad and considered her answer.

"Only when you begin to see the light will darkness lift and your heart be free. Listen to what your heart is saying..."

Cat sighed and stopped listening altogether.

• • •

Maya pressed her hands tightly together to stop them from shaking. They'd started quivering when the cardie-wearing woman had gazed up at her from the intricately illustrated tarot cards and said that she could see that Maya was a private person who kept her emotions very much to herself. That much was true.

Her hands had continued to shake when the smiling woman pointed out that friends were very important to Maya, that she often acted as referee between them, that her home life was sometimes a little bit oppressive, that she was academically gifted but that her real passion was for something artistic, and that she'd only just found this outlet in the last few months.

This accuracy was getting spooky.

Of course, she could have seen me taking photos before Cat snatched my camera away, Maya tried to tell herself. But that didn't explain how this woman could be so spot on about all the rest. Spooky wasn't a word that Maya used a lot, but it was definitely the one that was most appropriate now.

She'd been particularly interested when the woman said she saw that Maya was very fond of a young boy (it had to be Ravi, her sweet little brother), but there was also a younger girl around, one who seemed to bear her malice. ("Always keep an eye on her; for some reason she likes to see you fail," the psychic had said. Maya already did watch her thirteen-year-old sister, Sunny, like a hawk – the warning seemed apt.)

"Now *this* is an exciting card," said the tarot-reader, pointing to a dark-cloaked figure whose face couldn't be made out, and nodding wisely. "The death card."

Maya's nails dug into her palm in an involuntary spasm. That couldn't exactly be good news, could it?

"The death card doesn't have any bad implications, you know," the woman assured Maya, registering the alarm in her face. "It just means the end of one phase of your life and the start of a new one. It's all about change."

Maya smiled nervously.

"And the way it's positioned beside *this* card..." the tarot-reader tapped a neighbouring card with a fairy-type figure on it "...is very significant. Yes, there's a change coming and it's all to do with love..."

● ● ●

"Maya's taking for *ever*," moaned Cat.

"Well, it gives you more time to stuff your face, doesn't it?" said Sonja.

Cat gave her cousin a narrow-eyed glare across the canteen table, then helped herself to another chunk of carrot cake from the paper plate in front of her.

"Mind you, she has been there a long time..." Kerry muttered looking down at her watch.

The other girls had all had time for coffee (and cake, in Cat's case) and commiserations over their various lacklustre glimpses into the future, and *still* there was no sign of Maya.

"I'll go and have a nosy out in the hall – see what's happening with her," Anna suggested, rising from her chair.

"No need," Sonja nodded towards the glass-panelled door that opened into the main hall. "Here she comes now."

"Uh-oh," mumbled Cat through a mouthful of carrot cake. "By the look on her face, I think she needs to sit down – sharpish!"

CHAPTER 2

• •

ALL EYES ON OLLIE

"Don't look now, but I think we're being eyed up..."

Although the wonky clock on the wall of the End-of-the-Line café said it was ten to eight, it was actually 2.40 pm, and Nick was twenty minutes away from closing up this Sunday afternoon. In the background, the wonky jukebox was vibrating to the sound of some ancient Rolling Stones track, even though Joe had actually pressed the buttons for a Blur tune, which was just about the most up-to-date band Nick had deigned to put in his prized, original '50s Wurlitzer.

Nick Stanton, the owner of the End-of-the-Line café, and Irene, one of the pensioners who helped out with a few shifts a week, pottered back and forth to the kitchen, tidying up in a leisurely fashion now that most of the customers had left.

Ollie had sloped off – with his Uncle Nick's blessing – to spend the last chunk of his shift talking to the rest of his band, who were all occupying the window booth. Apart from the fact that there wasn't enough work to keep all three of them occupied, Nick was happy to encourage band discussions; as The Loud's manager, it pleased him to see the lads' enthusiasm.

"Where are we not supposed to be looking?" Ollie hissed at Joe. "Surely you don't mean Sunny."

Having pulled up a stool at the end of the table when he joined them, Ollie had his back to the room. As far as he could remember, the only other table that was still occupied was one that Maya's sister, Sunita, was huddled round with a couple of her mates. He couldn't imagine that *they'd* be eyeing up him and his friends, or that Joe would make a big deal out of it.

"Who's Sunny?" asked Andy, who'd joined the band last and knew the least about the background to Ollie's crowd.

"Maya's younger sister," Billy, The Loud's guitarist, explained.

"Ah..." nodded Andy. He'd met Maya – as well

as Billy – when they'd joined the Downfield photography club the previous summer, and now that the connection had been pointed out, he could see the similarity between the two girls instantly.

"Shhh, they'll hear!" Joe tried to quieten them down. "No – I didn't mean Sunny; I meant one of those two girls sitting over by the jukebox..."

Matt, who'd never specialised in tact, stared straight over at the table Joe had indicated.

"You sure, Joe? They're not looking now..." he shrugged.

"Yeah – they're not looking *now* because you lot are all staring over at them," hissed Joe, wishing he'd never mentioned anything in the first place. "But the one with the dark bob and the pierced nose has been ogling for the past ten minutes."

"Which one of us do you think she fancies?" Billy grinned.

"Well not *you*, if she catches a whiff of that gear," Ollie teased him, looking at his football top. "Don't you ever get changed after your games?"

Billy lifted his arm and took a long whiff under his armpit.

"Ahhh...!" he exclaimed with a wide grin on his face.

"Yeeeeeeeeuch!" the other lads all moaned.

"What?" asked Billy, pretending not to understand why they were offended. "Nothing wrong with a bit of sweat! Very macho, that is..."

"Well, I wouldn't worry about your personal hygiene problem, Billy – it's probably Matt she's after," said Ollie, nodding his head towards his undeniably good-looking mate.

Matt Ryan was tall with almost Mediterranean colouring – dark hair, brown eyes and olive skin. His powers of attraction in the town of Winstead were practically legendary and, in the past, he had been guilty of taking advantage of the fact that girls fell for him left, right and centre. But all that had changed when he met Gabrielle; she was the first girl he thought he could get ever get serious about. It was just a pity she hadn't felt the same.

Since she'd finished with him at New Year, Matt had seemed a little dazed and confused when he was around any girls outside his group of friends.

"Not my type," he said, checking out the staring girl unselfconsciously.

"Matt, your type used to be *any* type!" Ollie laughed.

Matt nodded, a rueful smile playing on his lips, as if to say that time seemed long, long ago.

"Nah, she's not my type either," said Andy with a straight face.

The lads erupted completely.

Andy never made a big deal about it, but everyone knew he was gay. At the regular weekly gigs the boys played at the Railway Tavern just along the road, it had become a running joke among them that he was a total heartbreaker without even trying. Plenty of girls in the audience stood gazing adoringly at him as he plucked his bass, completely unaware that the nice-looking, skinny boy they were checking out wouldn't ever be interested in them as anything but friends, at best.

"You know, seriously, though," said Billy, whose general enthusiasm helped him see opportunities everywhere, "we really should get some flyers printed up for our Thursday night spots. Then we could hand them out to girls like those two when we came across them; it could really help boost the numbers."

"Yeah – great idea!" Ollie enthused. "Wonder if we could get some done for the Valentine do we're playing at Cat's college on Saturday night?'

"We'd never get it organised in time," Andy pointed out.

"Maybe, but Billy's right – it could get more people into the Railway Tavern," Ollie shrugged. "I'll tell Nick about it when he comes back through from the kitchen. We could leave flyers on all the tables in here at nights and weekends, and just let people know about us..."

"Oh, yeah, *great* idea," said Matt, with a touch of sarcasm in his voice. "Only how are you going to afford that? The pathetic fee you get from Derek at the Railway Tavern only *just* covers the cost of hiring the gear you use."

"Well, thanks for that note of doom and gloom, Matt," Ollie smiled wryly. "Anyway, you're not even *in* the band – so what do you know?"

Matt knew he was being wound up, but he could give as good as he got.

"Hey, I'm *only* the guy who mixes your sound *for nothing* and ferries all your hire stuff to and from Central Sounds every week *for nothing*. But if you know someone else who's willing to do the job, feel free to hire them instead..."

"There's people queuing up, mate – just queuing up!" Ollie grinned.

"Right, you two – take it outside if you're going to start a fight!'

Irene stood with her hands on her hips by their table, armed with a damp dishcloth and an indulgent smile for Ollie and his friends.

"Yes ma'am!" barked Ollie, shooting her a salute.

"Elbows up, lads – your table's the last one I've got to wipe down," she ordered brightly.

Five pairs of elbows immediately lifted into the air.

"Now, where are all your lovely lady friends today?" Irene chirruped as she wiped.

"They're all at some New Age show up in the city," said Ollie, arms aloft. "Didn't Anna mention it to you this week?"

"Now maybe she did..." Irene replied. "New Age – that's the trendy name for all that crystal ball gazing, isn't it?"

"Um, kind of..." said Ollie, thinking how Anna would wince to hear her favourite subject being summed up like that.

"Ooh, I don't know if I'd fancy that myself," said Irene with a little shudder. "Heaven knows what strange things those girls are being told..."

The boys glanced at each other and had to struggle to stop themselves from sniggering – it was so surreal, listening to Irene tut-tutting over some imagined weird goings-on the girls were involved with, while they were all holding their hands in air as if they'd just surrendered.

"All done – you can relax again, boys," said Irene and with one final sweep of her cloth she was off.

"Ooh, do you think the girls are involved in some black magic seance right now?" gasped

Matt, holding his clenched hands under his chin in mock fear.

"Mmm, yeah, I think Irene's got the wrong end of the stick there, hasn't she?" said Ollie. "As far as I know, Kerry was just up for buying some smelly candles or something at this fair."

"Aromatherapy stuff you mean," said Andy, being more specific.

"Maybe we should have asked her to get some of that for your grotty dressing room at the Railway Tavern," suggested Matt. "To take away that niff of sweaty bands and sour beer that's always in there..."

"Don't think anything'll shift that – that's years' worth of pongs in there," said Billy. "But what do you reckon? Do you think the girls will be getting into all that palm-reading stuff? All that 'I see a tall, dark stranger' gubbins?"

"Nobody'd better be saying that to Kerry or there'll be trouble!" Ollie laughed. "Eh, Joe?"

Joe looked distracted.

"Joe – what's up?" Ollie quizzed him.

"It's that girl again. She's *definitely* looking over..." said Joe, trying to work out why the staring girl seemed so familiar.

"Yeah?" said Ollie and made to turn in his chair.

Joe had given up hoping his friends would be

subtle and didn't even try to stop Ollie from gawping.

"You know something? It's *you* she's staring at, Ol," Joe told his best friend.

Ollie felt a little peculiar as his eyes locked with the radar gaze of the girl sitting next to the jukebox.

"She's probably mistaken me for Damon Albarn," he joked, turning back to his friends. "Happens *all* the time."

But joking apart, Ollie felt a shiver up his spine. It felt as if those dark eyes were boring a hole in his back.

CHAPTER 3

• •

BILLY GETS HIS HOPES UP

"Hey, Billy boy – what do you reckon to this?"

Nick slapped a pink piece of paper on the Formica table top, flopped down on to the seat opposite and waited for a response.

Billy looked at the A5 sheet and didn't know what to say. There was an old-fashioned drawing on it, of what Billy guessed was supposed to be a Bunny Girl, beside black printed words which read: 'Pretty Ladies – the Escort Agency for the discerning gentleman. Discretion guaranteed. Phone today on...'

Billy was stumped. Maybe Nick – with his ponytail 'n' bald spot combo, and penchant for old rock T-shirts – wasn't *every* girl's idea of a dream date, but he never seemed to have any difficulty turning on the charm and chatting up women in the Railway Tavern, when he wasn't busy watching his protégés play. So why did he need to get involved in something as seedy as an escort agency?

"Nick – call for you!" Anna shouted across the café, holding the receiver of the wall phone up in the air.

"'Scuse," said Nick, grabbing up the pink slip of paper and striding off.

Billy sank into the seat with relief. He'd broken out into a sweat wondering what to say that wasn't along the lines of, "What are you – a dirty old man?"

But he wasn't out of trouble yet; Nick could finish his call and be back over just as quickly, and there was still no sign of Ollie. Billy wished like crazy that he hadn't decided to take a detour to come and meet Ollie after he'd finished his shift. He should have just made his way straight to The Swan, as he did every Tuesday evening, ready for the band rehearsal in the back room of Ollie's folks' pub.

He tried to catch Anna's eye – to ask her if Ollie was nearly through in the kitchen – when he was saved by the arrival of Kerry and Sonja.

"What are you doing here? Isn't it your practice night tonight?" asked Sonja, slipping in beside him and pinching a crisp from his open packet.

"Yeah, it is," nodded Billy, offering the packet to Kerry. "I'm just waiting for Ollie. I thought I'd come by for him since I was visiting a mate round the corner."

Billy wondered if he should tell the girls about what Nick had shown him, but he decided to save it for Ollie. Nick was his uncle, after all.

"Here's Ollie now," Kerry found herself smiling as she watched him bound through from the doorway that led to the kitchen. It was always the same when she caught sight of her boyfriend, no matter how long they'd been going out. That strange sense of shyness and bliss all rolled into one tingly, happy feeling that bubbled up inside her.

"Hey, gorgeous," said Ollie, before burrowing his face into the dark reddish curls that hid Kerry's neck, half kissing, half tickling her.

"Get off!" she giggled, pushing him gently away.

"Come on, Sonja – your turn!" he joked, leaning over as if he was about to give her the same treatment.

"Don't you dare!" yelped Sonja, holding her friend at arm's length.

As he laughingly watched the two of them tussling, Billy's eyes were suddenly drawn beyond them, to the dark-haired girl with the pierced nose who was sitting by the jukebox with her mate. And just like Sunday – as Joe had pointed out – her eyes seemed glued to Ollie.

Weird, thought Billy, though he was still more agitated by Nick's sudden interest in the escort agency.

"Have the girls told you about their amazing psychic readings on Sunday?" Ollie distracted him by asking, now that the play fight was over.

"No," Billy shook his head.

"Don't worry – you haven't missed out on much," grinned Sonja. "The only amazing thing about them was how *bad* they all were."

"Yeah?" said Billy, without much surprise. He didn't believe in all that spiritual stuff anyway. He liked things straightforward, simple and up front.

"Well, they weren't *all* bad," Kerry reminded her best friend. "Maya's was pretty amazing!"

"How come?" Billy quizzed her, now intrigued.

Billy had a soft spot for Maya; had even asked her out on a date when he'd first known her, but it hadn't worked out. Maya didn't seem to see him as anything more than friend material. But while he wasn't holding his breath or losing sleep over it, Billy – a born optimist – often wondered if she'd change her mind at any point in the future. He certainly wouldn't complain if she did.

"It was really accurate about her family and her personality and everything..."

"Yeah, but skip to the interesting part, Kez!" urged Sonja.

"Well," said Kerry, her hazel eyes widening behind her wire-rimmed specs. "She was told that there's going to be a new chapter in her life – a big change – and it's all to do with love..."

"Really?" said Billy, raising his eyebrows.

Maybe, he thought to himself, *just maybe I shouldn't be so cynical about all this psychic stuff after all...*

CHAPTER 4

● ●

UNEXPECTED INVITATIONS

"Here – let me."

Billy reached over with his muscular arms and grabbed the developing fluid out of Maya's hands.

"Thanks," said Maya, though she'd easily have managed to move the big plastic container from the table herself.

Now that it and various other miscellaneous objects had been cleared off the surface, Maya could open the flat cardboard box with her name scrawled on it, take out the prints she'd blown up the previous Wednesday, spread them out and take a good long look.

"I didn't see these last week – they're great," Billy commented, appearing by her side again.

"Thanks," Maya repeated. "I don't know about that one though..."

She tapped her finger beside one black and white shot of an old lady feeding bread to the swans on the river.

"I think I should maybe have another go at printing it. I think I can get better definition on it."

"Looks pretty good to me just the way it is," said Billy.

"Thanks," Maya found herself saying for a third time.

What's with Billy? she wondered. She'd caught him staring at her loads of times since she'd arrived at photography club tonight.

Andy shuffled up beside them, brushing his black hair back with his hand, and looked closely at the print.

"Nah, Maya's right – she probably could get more contrast on that one," he nodded.

"True – and it's worth doing," chipped in another voice. "It's a great composition."

Maya could have sworn she heard Billy sigh; as if first Andy and now Alex McKay – the photography club tutor – contradicting his opinion was a real pain.

It has to be that, Maya reassured herself, unwilling to consider the possibility that Billy's sudden over-the-top attentions could have a more ominous meaning. But then a thought occured to her. She'd called in to the End on the way to photography club, where her ear had been bent non-stop by Cat. Her friend seemed totally obsessed by Maya's love prediction and had sat rattling off a list of potential boyfriends for her, working her way through most of the boys at St Marks and beyond.

What if... just *what if* Cat had been playing Cupid for Billy, all on account of that stupid reading?

It was one explanation for Billy's sudden doe-eyed attention – if he'd been encouraged by the meddling Ms Osgood.

It would be right up Cat's street to try and orchestrate something, Maya frowned to herself, only dimly aware of the three heads around her, studying her prints. *She did it with Rudi, so I don't see why she wouldn't try it again...*

Cat had tried to throw Maya and the Dutch boy together a couple of times; first at the Christmas Eve party at Enigma, when she'd told him Maya fancied him and encouraged him to spring a snog on her out of the blue. If that wasn't bad enough, Cat had also egged the poor lad on to ask for a request for Maya at the Railway Tavern one night. Maya's heart sank at the memory of Ollie booming down the microphone for all the pub to hear, dedicating a song to her, "with lots of love from Rudi".

Now, if Cat was playing the same trick with Billy, getting him all stirred up about something that wasn't going to happen, Maya would *really* be angry with her. She'd got over all that awkwardness last summer, having to let Billy know that all they could be was friends. It had worked out really well since then: seeing Billy once a week at the photography club, and plenty of other times too, since he'd joined The Loud and started to hang out at the café more. It was important to Maya that their relationship – as mates – was understood and comfortable.

If Cat risks that for the sake of matchmaking, I'll kill her, Maya vowed, unaware that Alex had asked her something.

"Well, Maya?"

"Um, sorry... what?"

"I was just saying, I'm surprised you haven't done more photos of the band," said Alex in his earthy Glaswegian tones.

"Our friend Ollie—" she began.

"He's the lead singer," Andy interrupted, for Alex's benefit.

"Anyway, our friend Ollie says he wants to wait till the band have got more of a following," Maya explained. "He says he doesn't want me to take pictures when the pub's half empty and it looks like they haven't got any fans."

It was partly true; it was what Ollie had once said to her. But the other reason Maya hadn't pushed to do more with The Loud yet was that she felt a little self-conscious about taking photos of a band that included two photographers – Billy and Andy – both of whom were pretty good behind a lens.

"Aw, it's not half empty – don't listen to her, Alex. We're popular, honest we are!" Billy suddenly protested. "You should come along sometime and see the band for yourself!"

"I'd love to," Alex surprised the boys by saying. "When are you playing next?"

"Um, well, tomorrow," said Andy, slightly sheepishly. "We play every Thursday night at the Railway Tavern."

"Tomorrow...? Yep, I might just be able to make that."

Billy and Andy had inane grins splattered across their faces. Maya could easily see why; Alex didn't act like a teacher, but as their tutor at the evening class – and one they all respected and liked – it felt like a bit of a coup to the lads that he was interested in what they were doing.

"But if I come tomorrow, I want a favour in return," said Alex, fixing all three with an earnest look.

"Yeah, whatever," Billy nodded enthusiastically. "What is it?"

"I'm having a belated flat-warming party on Saturday, now that I've *finally* got the place finished. I just thought it would be nice if everyone from the club could come along..."

Maya felt a surge of excitement at the unexpected invitation. She loved her friends, loved hanging out with them, but the idea of going to a party where there'd be lots of new people sounded great. A real change. And most of them would be older – Alex was twenty-seven, she remembered he'd told them once – which would be pretty interesting too.

But despite all that, Maya's loyalty to her mates tugged at her and she was just wondering if it would be too cheeky to ask if she could bring them all along when Andy and Billy let out a groan almost in unison.

"Aw, we can't make it on Saturday!" Andy sighed.

"We've got a gig for Valentine's Day," Billy continued. "What a pain it's the same night!"

"Yeah, why couldn't it have been on Valentine's Day proper?" shrugged Andy.

"Because it lands on a Monday this year," Billy pointed out. "And no one would've come."

"Ah, well, never mind," Alex shrugged.

Wait a minute, thought Maya. *Just because the boys are playing a gig doesn't mean I can't go!*

"*I'd* still love to come," she found herself saying. "What time is everyone turning up?"

Even though she was looking up into Alex's face, Maya could sense the surprised stares Billy and Andy were giving her.

"Maya – I thought you were coming to see us on Saturday..." Billy said lamely.

"Hey, I'm sure The Loud can do without me in the audience for one night!" she said brightly.

And it won't hurt to nip this situation with Billy in the bud either, she figured.

If he was going slushy on her again, the last place Maya wanted to be was at a Valentine party with him – there was just too much opportunity for him to say or do something they'd both regret.

"Good!" exclaimed Alex, in his husky burr. "I'm glad you'll be able to make it, Maya!"

"So am I!" she smiled, ignoring the look of disappointment on Billy's face.

CHAPTER 5

• •

NUMBER ONE FAN

"It won't be the same if you don't come on Saturday!" said Kerry, gazing at Maya forlornly.

"Yeah, traitor!" laughed Sonja.

"Look, I'm here tonight to support the boys – I'm here *every* Thursday – so it's no big deal, is it?" Maya protested.

"*Could* be," Cat's voice came from above as she transferred full glasses from the tray she was carrying on to the table. "Could be a *very* big deal, depending what this Alex of yours is like..."

"What do you mean exactly?" Maya demanded. If Alex was going to turn up at the Railway Tavern tonight – and there was no guarantee that he definitely would; he'd only said he *might* come – the last thing Maya wanted was for Cat to be on her worst behaviour.

"Well," said Cat, settling herself down on a stool and continuing with her theory, totally unfazed by Maya's stern tone, "hasn't it crossed your mind that maybe *he's* the one?"

"*He* is my tutor at photography club. *He* is not the one," Maya said firmly. "And while we're on the subject of my stupid tarot reading, have you said something to Billy?"

"Me? Billy? What have I said?" Cat asked with a genuinely innocent expression on her face.

Though knowing Cat, that doesn't mean much... thought Maya.

"Billy. Did you tell him—"

"Uh-oh, don't look now, girls, but here comes Mr Sleazy," Cat burst in with a snigger.

Cat, Maya and Kerry were all facing the right way, but Sonja and Anna had to turn round in their seats to take a look at Nick, who'd just walked in with Derek, the owner of the Railway Tavern.

"I'm sure it's all just some mistake," said Anna, trying hard to think of an excuse that would make sense of the saucy advert her boss had been flashing about in the café the other day. By now, they'd *all* heard about Nick and the escort agency.

"Urgh, I doubt it," Cat shuddered. "I still can't believe what he's up to; and to think he used to go out with my mum!"

And to think you once told us you were his secret girlfriend, thought Maya, remembering the bizarre lie Cat had once come out with, just to get everyone's attention. But it had been at a bad time in Cat's life and Maya wasn't going to be so mean as to drag it up now.

What Maya *also* wasn't going to do – she knew – was get any sense out of Cat about Billy. That would have to wait till later. Alex had just arrived.

• • •

It was the last song in their set and Ollie was relieved when he cast a glance into the audience and saw that the staring girl had gone.

She was the same one who had been in the End – the one Joe had pointed out. She was easy to recognise with her dark helmet of shiny, bobbed hair and the sparkle of the diamanté stud in her nose. And, up till now, she'd been standing at the front of the watching crowd, at the very edge of the stage, her eyes locked on him.

There was no denying it had put him off; he knew he wasn't singing his best.

C'mon, Ol, he told himself now that she'd vanished. *Make this a good one to finish with...*

Ollie closed his eyes and let his voice soar above

44

Billy's guitar. Feeling more like himself, he hit the very last note, then heard the cheering and clapping begin.

"Thanks – see you next week!" he grinned out into the sea of faces and strode off, leading the other lads off the stage.

"Nice one!" said Nick, holding open the door to the corridor that led through to the small, dingy, backstage changing room. The band always headed straight there when they finished a gig; to wind down, catch their breath and have a quick post-mortem before they went back out to the bar and relaxed with their friends.

"Thanks, Nick. I lost it for a while there, but I think I pulled it together at the end," Ollie gasped, his heart still racing.

"And that's the one they'll go home remembering," Nick reassured him as they walked side by side along the corridor. "Hey, listen, I meant to show you something..."

Ollie gulped as he saw Nick pull out a pink piece of paper from his top pocket. He'd heard all about it from Billy, of course, but he hadn't managed to bring up the subject of what Nick thought he was doing using an escort agency; Dorothy or Irene were always around at work and it didn't seem like a great idea to talk about his uncle's dubious new hobby in front of the two old dears.

Of course, the other reason he'd said nothing was that the very idea filled him with dread. For all his apparent confidence, Ollie hated confrontation; he'd willingly do anything for an easy life, including avoiding awkward situations. With hindsight, he knew that he was partly to blame for the hiccup that had happened a few months before in his relationship with Kerry. She had been getting herself in a tangle of worries that she'd been too shy to tell him about, and he hadn't helped by seeing that something was wrong, but keeping quiet and hoping it would all be OK.

Now he faced the same situation with Nick – which was grossing out the girls as well as the guys in the band – and that feeling of dread was back in the pit of his stomach. He had to say or do something and maybe he'd fall out with his uncle over it. Or maybe it wasn't even his business...

Nick began unfolding the crumpled pink paper, while at the same time leaning on the dressing room door to open it.

"I just thought this was something you'd be interested in," said Nick as the door swung open.

I doubt it, Ollie thought in a panic, spotting the sexy drawing Billy had described to him. Behind him, in the corridor, he knew all the other lads would be hanging on his every word, waiting to see what he'd say.

"Well, each to his own, Nick," Ollie finally managed, shrugging apologetically as he strode into the cramped, messy room, "but this kind of thing doesn't really do it for me..."

Ollie stopped suddenly in surprise and felt Joe stumble into his back with a gasped "Ouff!"

Sitting cross-legged on the floor were two girls; one fair-haired and bored, one dark-haired and intense.

"Hi," said the intense one, looking straight at Ollie.

"Er, hi..." Ollie muttered in reply.

The girl with the pierced nose lost the intense look for a second and gave him a shy little smile.

CHAPTER 6

● ●

CAT PUSHES IT

"I suppose it's kind of sweet."

"Sweet, Joe? How do you figure that one out?" Matt asked, through a mouthful of spaghetti bolognese. The End provided most of Matt's nutritional needs; it certainly beat sitting alone at home in the sterile kitchen of his dad's huge house with only a Pot Noodle and the radio for company.

"Well, she's The Loud's first proper fan..." Joe shrugged, sounding unconvinced.

"First proper nutter, more like!"

"Hey, that's not really fair, Matt!" Ollie jumped in.

"Yep," nodded Matt, warming to his theme, "she's The Loud's first groupie."

Ollie sighed. He felt mean moaning about the

staring girl, but he couldn't help it. He'd felt terrible the night before at the Railway Tavern when Nick had shooed the girl and her friend out of the dressing room as soon as she'd waffled her piece about wanting to tell the band in person how great they were.

"Course it's fair!" said Matt, pausing for a second to suck a rogue strand of spaghetti into his mouth. "I mean, sneaking around backstage waiting for you to come off? That's too much – she could have just waited and told you how much she liked the band when you guys came out front, like any normal person would. And the looks she was giving you when you finally did come to hang around out in the bar with us... She's weird, man. I'm telling you."

Ollie knew exactly what Matt meant about the looks; the dark-haired girl's eyes had felt like lasers trained on him as he was introduced to Alex – Billy, Andy and Maya's photography tutor bloke. As he chatted to Alex, he'd seen her leaning against the far wall out of the corner of his eye, her reluctant friend still in tow.

Half of him dreaded her coming over and trying to speak to him again, but half of him would have preferred it – and at least it would have felt a bit more normal.

But whatever Ollie thought, he wasn't going to

admit it out loud – that would have made it seem too real. All he wanted to do was change the subject and forget the whole thing.

She might not even come back to see us play again, he tried to reassure himself, while denying the fact that he jumped every time the bell on the door of the café tinkled.

"Wonder where Kerry and the others are?" he said, glancing up pointlessly at the wonky clock above the jukebox. "Thought they'd be here by now."

"Don't change the subject," said Matt, pushing his empty plate away and giving a contented burp. "Admit it – you *do* think she's weird."

"OK, so she stares a lot, but that's not a crime is it? You can't exactly run to the police and say 'Help me, officer, a pretty girl's been staring at me a bit', can you?" Ollie tried to joke.

"She's not some girl who stares, Ol," Matt insisted. "She's a stalker. I bet you."

"Stalker Girl..." Joe muttered absently under his breath.

Ollie knew this bit of teasing was going to run and run. And from Matt's sudden grin, he knew he'd heard a nickname that was going to stick.

• • •

Sonja sat in the padded window seat of her bedroom, watching as her three friends wriggled in and out of a pile of clothes that were spread out on her bed.

"What do you think?" said Cat, pulling a creamy peasant top over her big boobs.

"Nah," said Sonja as Maya and Kerry crinkled up their noses. "That's an Anna top – it's too tame and hippy-dippy for you, Cat."

Cat yanked the top over her head and chucked it at Sonja, who caught it neatly and rammed it into an already stuffed carrier bag.

The girls were round at Sonja's early that Friday night after she'd put in an emergency call to them all. Her big sisters, Karin and Lottie – who had great taste in clothes – were having a radical clear-out of their wardrobes.

After pulling out a couple of tops for herself, Sonja did what any good friend would do and alerted her mates to the fact that they had one chance, and one chance only, to rummage through her sisters' cast-offs before they were taken in bin bags to the charity shop.

Anna – who out of all the girls could have benefited most from this free-for-all – was stuck doing a shift down at the End as usual. Ever mindful of the fact that their friend had minimal money and no parents around to treat her to new clothes, the girls were all conferring about what might suit Anna, with her pale skin and long, mid-brown hair. They were looking forward to seeing her face when they surprised her with the bag of goodies later on.

"Here's another Anna number," said Kerry, holding a long, pale-green cotton slip-dress up against her.

"It'd look pretty on you, too," Maya pointed out.

"Do you think so?" asked Kerry, stepping over towards the full-length mirror.

"Yeah, go on, try it on," Sonja encouraged her. "And anyway, I meant to ask, Kez – has Ollie said anything yet to Nick about him and the Lusty Ladies or whatever that dodgy escort outfit was called?"

"No," came Kerry's muffled reply as she gingerly eased off her button-fronted top; her broken collarbone was still in need of TLC. "He says he hasn't had a chance."

"God, Ollie can be such a chicken!" said Cat, pulling another top out of the muddle of clothes. "*I'll* ask Nick what he's up to – *I'm* not scared."

"No, you will not," warned Maya. Nick wasn't overly fond of Cat since all the nonsense that had happened with her the year before. Everyone – except Cat, it seemed – guessed that he only really tolerated her these days because of his fondness for Ollie and the rest of the crowd.

"It's difficult for Ollie, remember," Kerry tried to explain as Maya came to her aid and helped her step into the green dress. "Nick's his uncle *and* his boss..."

"That's never stopped Ollie being cheeky to him before," Cat pointed out.

"Yeah, but this is a pretty dodgy area we're talking about," said Sonja, exchanging looks with Kerry. Both of them could remember the last time Ollie and his uncle had had a run-in – when Ollie had believed Cat when she'd told him that Nick was messing her about. It wasn't true, of course, and the experience had been a horrible one for both uncle and nephew.

"Hey, maybe those girls in The Loud's dressing room last night were actually there to see Nick!" said Cat excitedly.

"What?!" said the other three in unison, wondering where Cat's flight of fancy was taking her.

"Well, Andy said Nick got the pair of them out of there pretty fast – what if they were escort girls, come to see him?" Cat suggested with her eyes wide. "*Then* he got embarrassed 'cause all the boys were in the room and ordered the girls out – to save face!"

"Cat," said Sonja, staring long and hard at her cousin, "if that's the case, why was Nick trying to show Ollie the ad about the escort agency just seconds before he opened the door? *That* blows your stupid theory..."

"And Joe told me that when he thought about it, he realised the dark-haired girl's been coming to see the band for ages," Maya chipped in, with another fact to destroy Cat's bizarre suggestion.

"These girls hanging round the band – they're not getting on your wick, are they, Kez?" Sonja asked, suddenly aware that it might be hard for her best mate to cope with the female attention the band was suddenly getting.

Kerry, who was now staring unhappily at the way the cotton dress was pulling unflatteringly across her hips, shook her head.

"No – they're just fans. It's what you expect with groups, isn't it?" she shrugged. "And anyway, it's not like Ollie or any of the lads are going to take advantage, are they?"

"True. By the way, that's too tight for you round the bum, Kez," Cat interrupted bluntly, even though her own white T-shirt was at least one size two small for her double D-cup figure. "Hey, why don't *you* try that dress, Maya? Might be just the thing for this party you're deserting us for tomorrow night..."

Maya had been wondering when the wind-up would start. It had taken Cat longer to get round to the subject than she'd expected.

"No, I don't want to go all dressed up; I'm just going to wear my black cropped trousers and that long-sleeved striped top I bought last week. It's not like it's any big deal – just a flat-warming."

"No big deal! Who's to say what could happen or who you might meet... if you haven't met him already, that is!" said Cat provocatively.

"Look, Cat," Maya warned her, "stop going on about Alex that way. It's really annoying. And it's not going to happen – all right?"

"Why not? He seemed really nice when we met him last night – a bit old, of course, and a bit too lanky for my liking. But if destiny is calling..."

"Cat – you're more obsessed with this stupid tarot thing than I am!" snapped Maya. "But while we're on the subject – did you say something to Billy about it?"

"No!" Cat shook her head indignantly. "I told you last night that I didn't."

"Well, I don't know if I believe you, since he seems to have gone all mushy on me in the last few days. Are you sure you haven't been playing your stupid little matchmaking games again?"

Sonja bit her lip. It had crossed her mind when she and Kerry had been gabbing on about the

Psychic Fair in the End on Tuesday that Billy seemed a little *too* interested in Maya's reading. Obviously, he thought it might be the right time to make another play for Maya...

"Cat hasn't said anything, honestly," said Sonja, coming to her cousin's rescue even though she was feeling cross with her. Cat was in one of her typically insensitive moods, where she was bound to open her mouth and fall out with someone before the night was over.

Maya didn't look convinced, but took Sonja's word for it.

"OK, so I got it wrong. Sorry, Cat," Maya apologised. "Maybe I got it wrong about Billy too. It's probably just my imagination."

"Or maybe it's just fate *making* you notice him..." said Cat, unaware that she was pushing it.

"Cat!"

Maya's irritated tone finally hit home.

"OK! OK!" said Cat, holding her hands up in an attempt to pacify. "So you're not going to find true love with Billy!"

Maya nodded, then turned to unzip Kerry.

"Or Alex," Cat couldn't resist adding.

Biting her lip, Maya decided to ignore her irritating friend.

"But *maybe*," Cat grinned wickedly, "you'll find Mr Right at this party tomorrow anyway!"

Sighing a long, deep sigh, Maya rolled her eyes at the very suggestion. But deep inside, she had to admit, she'd been thinking the very same thing.

CHAPTER 7

●●●●●●●●●●●●●●●●●●●●●●●●●●●●

HEARTS AND FLOWERS

Cat sounded hoarse when she came back over to join the other girls. But it wasn't a great surprise, considering they'd just seen her howling her head off to The Loud's version of Robbie's *Angels*, along with about six other girls from her beauty course.

"Sorry to leave you for so long, but I had to mingle," Cat apologised croakily, above the sound of the boys picking up the pace and launching into the Cardigans' *Lovefool*. "But are you having a good time?"

"Course we are!" said Sonja, dancing to the music. "This hall makes a brilliant venue. They should put more gigs and stuff on in here."

"I know, that's what my friend Vikki says," Cat nodded, gazing around Winstead College of Further Education's roomy auditorium. "She's on the student committee and she's really pushing for more to happen."

"Were the committee in charge of doing this place up?" asked Kerry, gawping at the huge cloth banners, decorated with hearts, that covered acres of the white-painted breeze-block walls. "Apart from the stage, I wouldn't recognise it as the same place you lot put on the pantomime at Christmas!"

"I know – it's great, isn't it?" Cat nodded with pride. She was really enjoying showing off the college to her mates. Even though they said they were behind her, she sometimes felt she had to justify why she hadn't stayed on at St Marks to do her A levels and prove to them that she hadn't just chosen her course on a whim.

Which, of course – being Cat – she more or less had.

"Isn't that Vikki coming over now?" Anna motioned to the smiling girl making her way over towards them.

The only other time Cat's friends had seen Vikki was when she was swathed in pink netting, playing Fairy Godmother to Cat's Cinderella in the college charity panto they'd both starred in. But even out of costume, there was no mistaking Vikki; she was a big girl, in both size and personality, and radiated charisma.

"Hi!" she boomed, jangling rows of multicoloured metal bracelets against her brown skin as she waved. "Hey, Cat – these boys of yours are great. I'm glad you told me I should book them!"

Vikki nodded her head in the direction of the stage, where – for the last hour and a half – The Loud had been belting out a range of love-related covers for the night's Valentine theme.

"Told you! And wait till Matt starts DJing – if anyone's still not dancing by then, Matt'll get them going!" Cat grinned.

"Sounds good to me!" said Vikki, slapping her hands together.

"Hey, and Vik," added Cat, "my friends here were just saying how amazing the hall looks with all the banners and everything."

"Definitely!" Sonja agreed, while Anna nodded positively at her side.

"And I like the little touches too," Kerry chipped in enthusiastically. "Like the bunch of pink roses tied around Ollie's mike."

Kerry had loved that; seeing her boyfriend crooning with those flowers tangled all around the metal stand, tied with a big satin ribbon. She wished Maya was here with her camera instead of at her tutor's party – it would have been the perfect photo opportunity.

"Oh, I'll happily take credit for everything else

tonight, but I didn't do *that*," laughed Vikki. "The guys in the band must have come up with *that* gimmick themselves."

Kerry frowned. Ollie would have mentioned it if they'd planned something, wouldn't he?

Unless Nick came up with the flowers as a last minute thing...? she wondered, then instantly dismissed the idea.

As their manager, he'd do anything to push the lads' career on, but there was as much chance of Nick the old rocker dreaming up the notion of roses and ribbons as there was of him announcing that B*witched were his favourite band.

● ● ●

Ollie stepped away from the mike for a second as the band broke into an instrumental section.

"Check out Nick, stage left," said Billy, leaning over to whisper the information fleetingly in Ollie's ear.

Trying to be subtle, Ollie moved his head from side to side in time to the music and managed to catch a glimpse of his uncle standing in the wings – with a woman snuggled up very close to him.

Is she *from that escort agency?* Ollie's mind whirred, wondering why his uncle would phone up a dodgy agency and bring whoever they'd sent him along as a date to their *gig*, for God's sake...

Although he hadn't said so to the others yet, Ollie had already made up his mind to avoid bringing up the whole subject with Nick. His uncle's private life was his own business, he'd decided, and as long as Nick didn't try and drag out that stupid ad for Ollie to look at again, the matter was dropped. But now tonight, this made a difference – it was embarrassing.

Ollie glanced around again and found his worst fears were confirmed: the woman certainly seemed tarty enough to come from some seedy agency, with her tight leopard-skin jacket, layers of gold chains and a ton of heavy make-up.

What the hell's Nick playing at? Ollie fretted as he grabbed hold of the microphone stand – aware for a second of a sharp pain in the palm of his hand – and launched back into the song.

It was only as the track – and the whole set – ended, that he was able to glance down and see what was wrong. Holding his hand up, while the roars of the crowd erupted in front of him, Ollie instantly spotted the rose thorn embedded in his skin.

"You all right?" Billy shouted above the clamouring, from a few feet away.

"Yeah, no problem," Ollie grinned back, while

making a mental note to advise the organisers to try carnations, or lilies, or even *dandelions* next time they wanted to dress up the stage for gigs. Anything but roses with their surprise spikes.

Saying a heartfelt "thanks!" again into the microphone before the band left the stage, Ollie was hit by a sudden wave of inspiration. Tugging at the satin ribbon, he freed the flowers, and with a dramatic sweep of his arm, threw the bundle of pink roses out into the audience.

His triumphant smile wavered, however, as he saw one girl near the front of the stage leap into the air and grab the floral missile.

Her diamanté nose stud twinkling in the light, Stalker Girl held the roses in her hands and inhaled the scented petals of her prize.

• • •

"Nice these, aren't they?"

Maya turned away from the amazing black and white images on the walls of the flat and smiled at the stranger.

"Yes. Alex told me about these photos of his, but it's great to actually see them."

"So," smiled the stranger, handing her one of two glasses of red wine he held. "How do you know Alex then?"

Maya was momentarily confused; why had he given her this drink? She hadn't asked for one – only recognised his face vaguely from some conversation she'd passed earlier in the hall – and she never touched alcohol.

Just as she was about to refuse the wine, it dawned on Maya that she was being chatted up. In the circumstances – and this being one of Alex's friends – it seemed churlish to refuse; she'd just hold on to the glass till she got an opportunity to put it down somewhere.

"Well, I know Alex through the photography club he runs," she explained.

"Oh, do you teach at Downfield too?"

Maya felt a ripple of pleasure at the compliment.

"No, no – I'm at college. I go to St Mark's sixth form. Do you know it?" she grinned.

"Er, no, no I don't!"

Maya liked the way he laughed at his mistake. His eyes crinkled and a dimple dented either cheek.

Two twinkling brown eyes stared intently into hers. For a split second, Maya thought of Cat and of her suggestion that Maya might meet someone special at this party...

Don't be stupid! she scolded herself. *One nice-looking guy talks to you for all of five seconds and you start believing all that rubbish about destiny...*

"I'm Maya, by the way," she continued, feeling slightly shy all of a sudden.

"I'm Sam."

He smiled and gave her another glimpse of those dimples.

"And how do *you* know Alex?" Maya asked, smiling encouragingly.

"I used to share a flat with him, along with another couple of mates," Sam replied. "Before he turned all yuppie and got himself a mortgage and a place of his own."

Maya took another glance around the living room: with its cool blue walls – hung with Alex's own dramatic photographs – and two long, low, denim-coloured sofas, it seemed perfect.

"You're not jealous, are you?" she joked.

"Jealous?" said Sam, looking her up and down slowly. "A great flat, a beautiful 'pupil' hanging round that flat – of *course* I'm jealous!"

Another ripple shot down Maya's spine, but not of pleasure, this time. With a fixed smile on her face, she shook her head a little in confusion. Surely she couldn't have got him *that* wrong. Surely he couldn't be *that* much of a creep...

"Well, I'm not exactly 'hanging around' – I've only come to the party because I was asked," she replied, with a touch of iciness to her voice.

"I *bet* you were," Sam smirked suggestively. "So,

hasn't Alex asked you to pose for him yet? I know *I* would if I was any good with a camera..."

"You– you're interested in photography?" Maya found herself asking, though she knew perfectly well that he wasn't. She just wasn't sure how do deal with this – up until now, everyone Alex had introduced her to had seemed really nice. Now here was a friend, an ex-flatmate of Alex's, coming on to her like a total lech, and she didn't know what to do.

"Maya!"

It had been a long time since she'd been so relieved to hear her name called.

Ashleigh and Jane – the only two others from photography club who'd bothered to come – were waving her over to join them.

"Sorry," she said to Sam, although she wasn't.

"Didn't mean to drag you away," Ashleigh shrugged when Maya joined them by the fireplace.

"Don't worry – honestly," said Maya, sticking the full glass of wine up on the marble-topped mantelpiece. "What's up?"

"Me and Jane are thinking of heading off," Ashleigh whispered, pulling an apologetic face. "We just wondered if you wanted to come."

"But we haven't been here long!" Maya replied. Despite her most recent encounter, she was still buzzing from being at this party, in this great flat, with all these new, older people to get to know. It certainly wasn't like one of Matt's lairy, free-for-all house parties.

"Yeah, I know, but it's not really..." Ashleigh pulled another face and glanced at Jane as she tried to find the right word, "...our scene, is it?"

Maya felt slightly irritated for Alex's sake. He didn't *have* to invite his students to his party, and yet when he did, only three of them turned up. And two of *those* were about to leave after one sip of cider and a handful of peanuts.

"Well, whatever..." shrugged Maya. She knew she didn't have a right to be annoyed with Ashleigh and Jane if they didn't feel comfortable. "But I'm going to hang around for a while."

"Tell Alex bye from us," said Jane, pulling her bag up on to her shoulder.

Maya looked over towards the crowd of people in the kitchen – she could hear their tutor's gravelly Glaswegian voice from where she stood and see his lanky frame towering over the huddle of friends he was talking to.

"Why don't you tell him yourself? He's only through there," she motioned to the girls.

Ashleigh and Jane both shuffled awkwardly; it was obvious that they felt out of place and would be relieved to go.

"OK, OK," said Maya, sensing their discomfort. "I'll tell him for you."

"Thanks, Maya!" they both grinned at her.

"See you on Wednesday then..."

"Yeah, bye!"

Maya watched as they made their getaway. If she hadn't been so disappointed in them it would have been funny. Both Jane and Ashleigh had turned from sensible sixteen-year-olds into shy little schoolgirls as soon as they stepped through the front door, viewing Alex's other guests – who were all in their twenties – as if they were aliens.

• • •

They'd felt out of place from the word go, but Maya had found it exciting to be introduced to Alex's friends and had loved nosying around the flat, and seeing the work that Alex had done. Even here on the mantelpiece, there was a beautiful framed photograph of pretty girl on a hill with a dark, thunder-filled sky behind her.

Maya was just studying it, wondering who the girl was, when a familiar voice interrupted her thoughts.

"All alone again?"

Sam's eyes were roaming all over her once more as his elbow struggled to find the mantelpiece.

"Mmmm," murmured Maya non-committally, suddenly wishing she *had* scuttled off with the girls.

"Well, it just gives me a chance to get to know you better, doesn't it?" he grinned at her. "Here's to us getting more friendly – cheers!"

With that, Sam clattered, rather than clinked, his glass on Maya's untouched one, still resting on the mantelpiece. The force of his toast sent the drink, and the framed photo of the girl, flying... landing with a conversation-stopping smash of glass on the polished wooden floor.

"Sam – leave it!"

Alex pulled his friend away from the splinters as Sam uselessly and drunkenly swayed forward to pick them up.

"Sorry... sorry..." muttered Sam, moving away slowly towards the kitchen. Another guy appeared at his side and steered him away from the mess he'd made.

"Are you all right? You didn't get cut by flying glass or anything, did you?" asked Alex with concern, crouching down to join Maya on the floor.

"No, I'm fine," she reassured him, gathering up shards of glass. Her gaze landed on a decorative ceramic bowl in the fireplace. "Should we just put the glass in this for the moment?"

"Good idea," said Alex, gingerly dropping chunks of broken wine glass into it. "I'm sorry about Sam – he's such an idiot. He always says he won't get drunk and then he does."

"I didn't even realise he was drunk when I was first talking to him," Maya admitted, holding the silver-framed photo over the bowl and delicately brushing off the splinters so they didn't scratch the picture any more than it already was.

"Yeah, he hides it well, but you always know he's had too much when he starts making a fool of himself, like now," shrugged Alex sadly. "He's a nice bloke when he's just sticking to coffee. Which reminds me..." Alex raised his head and looked over towards the kitchen.

"...Simon, Melanie, could one of you stick the kettle on and try and get some coffee down Sam's neck? Or make him eat something – that should sober him up a bit."

Up this close, it looked to Maya like Alex could do with eating something. She'd never noticed before how prominent his high cheekbones were: his grey-blue eyes, fringed with long, fair eyelashes, seemed more deep-set than she remembered.

"Oh, the picture got it too, did it?" Alex said sadly, turning his attention back to tidying.

He stretched his arm across the bowl and

reached out for the shattered frame that Maya was still holding.

For a second, his long, slender fingers overlapped her own.

For a second his eyes flickered up to meet hers.

For a second, she felt as if a bright, clear bolt of lightning had hit her.

Hard.

CHAPTER 8

● ●

SOMEONE'S WATCHING YOU...

"Roll on closing time, eh, Ollie?" grinned Anna as she swooped past him from the kitchen and zigzagged her way between the heaving tables with a loaded tray.

"Too right," Ollie called after her, quickly wiping down the coffee-ringed, stainless-steel counter top before slamming down another tray on to it. "Three o'clock can't come fast enough!"

It was still only midday and, so far this Sunday, work had been hectic. Ollie wasn't handling it too well; the combination of a café full of clamouring customers after a late night gigging at Winstead College was getting on top of him.

None of his other friends had turned up this morning, he noticed – their regular spot in the window booth was occupied by a family with

72

small, noisy children – and Ollie desperately envied the others their lie-ins.

"What have you got planned when you knock off?" asked Anna, swooping back with her now empty tray. She knew that Ollie rarely slowed down. If he wasn't beavering away in the End or Nick's record shop next door, he'd be helping at his parents' pub, working on music with the band, or up to his armpits in oil trying to get his broken-down Vespa to work. Somehow, he always managed plenty of time for Kerry in among it all – luckily for her.

"Nothing!" grinned Ollie. "Sweet, lying-flat-on-my-back nothing!"

"Ooh, I could do with a bit of that too, considering what time I finally got in from the college party last night," Anna laughed, slipping around the counter and heading back towards the kitchen.

She hesitated in the doorway as if a thought had just crossed her mind.

"By the way, have you noticed?" she whispered to him.

"What?" Ollie asked, panicking that he'd messed up an order. His brain was so mushy today, he wouldn't have been surprised if someone who'd been expecting eggs and sausage was sitting with a plate of toasted dishcloth in front of them.

"Don't look, but the table nearest the door – it's your little fan."

Ollie looked at Anna blankly as he tried to get his fluff-filled brain into gear.

"You know – *her*!" Anna whispered, eyes wide. "What does Matt call her? Stalker Girl!"

Ollie's eyes rolled over reluctantly towards the door, but he was relieved to see that the table was empty. Although at the back of his mind, he was dimly aware of hearing the bell above the door tinkle as it opened. Or closed...

"No one there now," he shrugged. "Are you sure it was her, Anna? You're as tired as I am, remember."

"Yes – I recognised the little nose stud," said Anna, squinting out into the street to see if she could spot the girl walking away. "Oh well, doesn't look like she's so interested in you any more..."

"Phew," sighed Ollie.

● ● ●

The last customer was still flicking through a Sunday paper, eating an apple pie, and seemed in no hurry to leave. But Nick didn't mind. He'd flipped over the 'Closed' sign ten minutes early to dissuade any latecomers and was sitting slumped on a stool at the counter with a steaming mug of tea in front of him.

Ollie stood with his elbows on the counter, staring off into the middle distance. Both of them were too tired to think about tidying up yet; a short breather was called for first.

"That was nice of you to let Anna knock off early" Ollie mumbled.

"Well, let's face it, Ol," said Nick with a yawn. "She was out as late as us last night, but she worked twice as hard as either of us today."

"True..." nodded Ollie. "Good night though, wasn't it?"

"Yep, you played a blinder," Nick nodded. "Eva thought so too."

Ollie's heart immediately sank – he'd forgotten all about Nick and his dubious date. After sticking his head round the dressing room door the previous night, Nick had vanished with 'Eva'.

"Nick...?"

Ollie's toes curled at the thought of what he was about to get into.

"Yeah?" said Nick absently, scratching the dark stubble on his chin.

"Who exactly is this... Eva woman?"

"Eva? What – you've never seen her down at the Railway Tavern before?"

God, it's worse than I thought, Ollie groaned inside. *He's been out with her before...*

"Er, no."

"You must have seen her – with Derek?"

"What, *Derek* goes out with her *too*?" Ollie winced. This was getting worse and worse. His uncle not only phoned up girls from an escort agency, but *shared* them with the manager of the Railway Tavern as well?

Jeez – what's he going to do next? Ollie worried. *Introduce me to his new girlfriend, Miss Whiplash, and tell me he got her number off a card left in a phone box?*

"Huh?" grunted Nick, furrowing his brow so much that his bushy eyebrows practically met in the middle. "What are you on about? Eva's Derek's wife. They both came along to your gig last night with a mate of theirs who runs the Balinard Hotel. He's looking for a band to do functions."

"But you disappeared..." said Ollie lamely.

"Yes – to talk business with them."

"But you never said..."

"Ol, I didn't know Derek was bringing this geezer down last night till he arrived with him, and I didn't want to mention anything to you lads until I got the chance to talk to him and see if he's up for it!"

"And is he?" said Ollie, suddenly excited by the idea of the band getting more bookings.

"Well, yeah, he is."

"But why didn't you say anything today?" Ollie queried, now wide awake.

"'Cause a) this place has been a madhouse from the minute we opened up, and b) he's not talking specifics until I go for a meeting with him tomorrow. OK?"

"OK!" grinned Ollie.

"And hold on a minute, sunshine," said Nick, narrowing his eyes at his nephew. "Let's rewind a bit here. What did you mean about Derek 'going out with Eva too'? Did you think I was seeing her or something?"

"Uh..." muttered Ollie, shuffling in his Nikes. "Well, kind of. I thought she was from that, um, escort agency place..."

"*What* escort agency place?" asked Nick, looking totally mystified.

"The one you've got that flyer for! The one you keep trying to get everyone interested in!" waffled Ollie, feeling his cheeks going pink.

Nick let his head slip back on his shoulders and let out a low groan.

"Ollie, you idiot," he sighed, bringing his gaze back down towards his nephew. "Derek knows someone in the printing game; I got a sample of the sort of flyers he does and a price off him."

"Flyers..." Ollie repeated, the truth finally sinking in.

"Yes," growled Nick. "You guys told me you're interested in getting flyers done for the band, so I sussed it out for you. And what do I get in return? You write me off as being some sleazebag who uses a dodgy escort agency!"

Ollie could see how irritated Nick was. Drastic action was needed.

"Only joking, Nick," he laughed unconvincingly. "Just a wind-up. 'Course I knew what you meant! Anyway, I'd better go and empty the bins out the back..."

He'd never moved so fast, shooting through the kitchen, grabbing the bulging black bag out of the plastic bin and slamming open the door to the yard in one fell swoop.

Wait till I tell the others! Ollie winced as he heaved the bag into the square wheelie bin. *There we were, thinking the worst of poor old Nick when—*

"Hey, Ol," came his uncle's voice from the kitchen's back door. "I've just had a weird message for you on the phone – some girl said to meet your girlfriend in the Plaza when you finish work..."

"Meet Kerry?" asked Ollie, perplexed. Kerry and her folks were supposed to be off doing some family visit somewhere today.

"I guess... But it wasn't her."

"So who was it that called?"

"Dunno. Didn't recognise the voice. And then they just hung up," replied Nick, leaning in the doorway.

"Didn't you ask?"

"No, I was in a rush. That guy was leaving and I was trying to lock up behind him."

"Didn't you do 1471?"

"Why would I do that? Listen Ol..." Nick frowned at him, "don't give me a hard time – you've done enough of that today so far, mate."

Running back inside the café, Ollie picked up the phone, dialled quickly and listened to the recorded message. "...The caller withheld their number."

Ollie's head was spinning. He'd only just solved one mystery and now here was another.

• • •

"Nah, she's *definitely* gone off to see her Auntie Wotsit," Sonja yawned down the phone at Ollie. "I spoke to her earlier, before she and her folks headed off."

She soon perked up though when Ollie explained about the mystery call.

"Gawd – what are you going to do, Ol?"

"I'm going to buzz the others first to see if they

know anything," he replied, moving out of the way of Nick's mopping. "And then I'm just going to head down to the Plaza anyway. I mean, maybe something happened; maybe she decided not to go to her auntie's after all..."

"Yeah, but that doesn't make sense, Ol – and it still doesn't explain who the message came from," Sonja reasoned.

"I know, I know... But what else can I do?"

But the hasty dial-around to the others drew a complete blank. Now, as he hurried to the Plaza, Ollie could feel his heart pummelling at a rate of knots.

Coming to a halt dead in the middle of the shopping centre, he put his hands on his hips and gazed all around him. There were a few Sunday shoppers about, though not many; a handful of people sat in the Plaza's café, a few more in Burger King. It was a cold Sunday in the middle of February and not many people had been tempted out. There weren't exactly crowds galore that could hide Kerry from view.

Panting, Ollie sat down on a seat for a second and tried to get things straight in his mind. He'd pretended to Nick that the misunderstanding about the escort ad was just a wind-up. Well, now it looked like *he* was being well and truly wound up by someone... But who?

Ollie couldn't handle mysteries: he liked things to be straightforward. So now, he decided, his phone call must've been the work of kids. Well, it made sense, didn't it? Crank calls were what kids sometimes did for kicks. He'd been guilty of it himself when he was younger.

A wild thought suddenly struck him: could Sunny be the culprit? Then he dismissed the idea – Maya's little sister and her giggly mates hadn't even been in the café today, so she wouldn't know Ollie was working the Sunday shift.

Kerry's at her aunt's and I should be home sticking my head under the shower, he told himself, standing up to go.

He didn't spot the dark-haired girl in the café window, watching him intently as he walked away.

CHAPTER 9

• •

PRESENT TENSE

Sunita's eyes skimmed over the envelope she held in her hands. Then, with a deft flick of her wrist, she flung it over the breakfast table at Maya.

"For you..." she sniffed haughtily, then slithered around the back of Maya's chair, pretending to busy herself at the sink.

Maya glanced down blankly at what the Monday morning post had brought her. Her mind wasn't on it; her mind wasn't on the uneaten breakfast in front of her either. The only thing her mind was on was how ridiculous it was to keep thinking about what happened on Saturday night. Especially since *nothing* happened.

"Anything interesting?" asked Nina Joshi, breezing into the kitchen and seeing the envelope in her daughter's hands.

"Um, I don't know..." Maya shook her head.

Slipping her finger under the paper flap, she tore open the envelope and stared at the card in front of her.

"A Valentine! How exciting!" smiled her mother, leaning over to look at the delicate fabric heart stuck to the front of it, while pulling on her jacket. "Any idea who it's from, Maya?"

"No," said Maya, numbly opening it up.

"You don't know it yet, but I'm the one...," came Sunny's voice over her shoulder, reading out the message inside.

Maya snapped the card closed. She didn't know who it was from, but she didn't want her sly little sister gawping at it.

"Does that give you any clues?" asked her mother with a gentle smile.

"No," Maya repeated.

She'd have said no even if the sender's identity was crystal clear; from everything they'd said as she was growing up, the concept of boyfriends was definitely frowned upon by her parents. At least while studying and exams came first. From her mum's reaction today, a silly, sweet Valentine was on the right side of Boyland. Any further and there could be problems.

She genuinely didn't have a clue who could have sent it. But she knew who she *wished* it was from...

• • •

"Awww..." cooed Cat, Sonja and Maya as they gazed at the contents of the unwrapped parcel on the Formica tabletop.

"And look at this! It's so sweet!"

Kerry held up a ring box, then snapped the lid back to reveal a single Loveheart sweet inside, with the message 'I love you' on it.

"Isn't that gorgeous? How long must it have taken Ollie to shop for all of this stuff, never mind wrap it all up!" Sonja gasped, holding up a silver ankle chain decorated with tiny hearts.

The girls had cooed endlessly over Ollie's many silly and slushy Valentine gifts for Kerry: a rose petal bath ball; a heart-shaped pencil sharpener; two heart-shaped hair clips made of shiny red stones; even little biscuit cutters that spelt out the word 'love'.

Joe found it hard to join in. It wasn't that he felt jealous of Kerry and Ollie and their show of affection; somehow the car accident had put that all into perspective for him, and that old, agonising longing for Kerry just wasn't there any more. It was just that the whole lovey-dovey gift thing and the girly cooing made him feel a bit...

Icky, was the word that came to mind.

The sight of Ollie walking down the road filled

him with relief. Even if the expression on his best mate's face didn't look exactly like that of a boy in a romantic mood.

"Ollie! Thank you!" smiled Kerry, wrapping her arms around her boyfriend as he slid into the seat next to her. "But you didn't have to post it – I thought we were just going to swap presents when we saw each other!"

With that, Kerry bent down and pulled a card and gift-wrapped present from her bag.

"Ah..." muttered Ollie, pursing up his face as if he'd just sucked mighty hard on a lemon.

"Ah, what?" Sonja, quizzed him.

"Then I guess this..." Ollie pulled a clip-framed picture out of an opened brown envelope, "...isn't from you..."

The girls and Joe all stared at the hand-made collage held together behind the glass. There were lots of musical elements to it: torn strips of old-fashioned sheet music were stuck to the backing paper; headlines like 'best singer in the world' and 'star attraction' had been ripped out of music magazines and stuck on too. But the central image – framed by a red tissue paper heart – was a Polaroid snapshot of Ollie holding on to a mike stand; a mike stand with pink roses wrapped round it.

"Where did you get this?" asked Kerry, feeling

herself shudder, even though the End was cosy and warm.

"It was outside the front door at home this morning, just propped up against the wall," said Ollie.

"Look – there're even real pink rose petals dotted about inside the frame," Cat pointed out. "The same as..."

"...those roses on the mike stand," Maya finished off the sentence for her.

"I tell you," Ollie shook his head, his face as white as a sheet, "this is really doing my head in. First, no one owns up to sticking those stupid flowers on stage on Saturday; then there's that wild goose chase to the Plaza to meet 'my girlfriend' yesterday, and now this. What's happening? Is there some weird configuration going on in my star sign or something?"

"More like some weird little fan getting obsessive about you," said Cat matter-of-factly. "Some psycho groupie wanting to get her claws into you."

"Aw, come on, Cat – that's a bit far-fetched," Ollie protested.

But he realised from the others' silence that they agreed with her.

"Cat could be right, Ol," Joe nodded. "Stalker Girl was at the gig on Saturday night – she could have stuck the flowers on your stand if she'd got to the hall early enough."

"*And* she was in here yesterday morning," Anna chipped in. The others hadn't noticed her wander over from wiping tables when Ollie dragged the picture out. "She could have heard us speaking about what you were going to do come closing time."

"This Polaroid was taken at Saturday's gig," said Sonja tapping the picture. "And these petals match the roses from there. Yep – I'd say Stalker Girl's your girl."

"Nah – it's just too mad," Ollie shook his head, giving Kerry's hand a reassuring squeeze. "I'm sure all this stuff isn't connected. There's got to be some other explanation."

"Oh, yeah – like what?" Cat dared him.

Ollie said nothing; he hadn't a clue. Only a really, really bad feeling...

CHAPTER 10

●●●●●●●●●●●●●●●●●●●●●●●●●●●

DEVELOPING FEELINGS

Maya was in deep denial. She *didn't* have feelings for Alex, or at least that's what she kept telling herself.

It's all Cat's fault, she fumed. *If she hadn't put the stupid idea of finding 'someone special' at the party into my head... if she hadn't forced me to go and get that ridiculous tarot card reading done in the first place...*

But mostly, Maya was infuriated with herself for letting Saturday night's non-event affect her like it had. She and Alex had been cleaning up the broken glass; their fingers had touched for half a millisecond; they both went back to chatting to people at the party; and Maya left about an hour later.

So why am I finding it so difficult to make eye

contact with him tonight? she chastised herself. *And why do I get the feeling that he's avoiding me?*

"Whoah there!" said Billy, coming up behind her and snatching her hands.

"What do you think you're doing?" she snapped, uncomfortable at finding her friend's arms wrapped around her and his chest pressed against her back.

The Valentine card – was it from Billy? she wondered fleetingly, remembering her recent suspicions.

"He's trying to stop you from slicing your fingers off!" said Andy, appearing at her side.

Maya stared down at the paper guillotine in front of her and the print she'd been about to trim. It was true; her fingers probably had been exactly where they shouldn't have been. She wasn't concentrating.

"Thanks – thanks, Billy," she said in a softer tone, gently wriggling herself out of his arms.

"That's OK," he replied, reluctantly letting her go.

"Hey, you two – Alex is trying to get your attention," Andy nudged them.

They spun their heads round in the direction Andy was pointing; everyone else in the room was facing the tutor.

"I was just saying to the others, there's a photography exhibition on at the gallery up in the city. It finishes this weekend and I thought maybe we should all go up as a group on Saturday and check it out."

Alex stood with his rangy shoulders slightly hunched as usual, as if the low roof was in danger of pressing down on his almost two metre frame.

He's not even my type... Maya tried to tell herself, her eyes automatically taking in the uniform of plain jeans and dull, short-sleeved shirt he nearly always wore, rain or shine.

Not that I have a type, she silently added. *But if I did, it wouldn't be him...*

"So who's up for it? Quick show of hands, yeah?"

Maya felt her hand slide traitorously into the air, before she'd even properly considered whether or not she could make it on Saturday.

"Aw, not again!" wailed Billy. "Me and Andy can't make it, Alex!"

"We've got tickets to the match!"

"No worries, guys," Alex shrugged. "It's just the way it goes. So, Jane, Stuart, Ashleigh, Salman, Martin... you're all up for it, yes? And I'll check with the others when they come out of the dark room."

What about me? Maya fretted, letting her hand slip waveringly back down again.

Alex turned and started checking out the sheet of contacts Salman was holding up.

Either I'm right and Alex is ignoring me, Maya realised with a shock, *or I'm going totally mad.*

CHAPTER 11

• •

THE COAST IS CLEAR

"She hasn't been in the End all week!"

"So?"

"Well, Cat, if she hasn't been in the café all
week, then she can't be much of a stalker!"

"And she's not turned up tonight so far," said
Joe, glancing round the busy pub. Even though he
didn't entirely share his mate's optimism, Joe felt
duty-bound to back him up – he knew Ollie felt
totally uncomfortable with the whole idea of this
weird 'groupie' girl hanging around, and with the
teasing he was getting from the likes of Cat and
Matt in particular.

"Early days, Ol, early days. You've still got ten
minutes before you go on stage," Matt grinned.
"So there's plenty of time for her to turn up
and present you with a fan photo and a box of

chocs, or whatever she's got up her sleeve next!"

"Duck, if something comes flying at you on stage, Ol," Cat cackled. "It'll probably be her knickers!"

"Cat!" said Ollie, disgust written all over his face. "What are you on about?"

"Well, all those middle-aged housewives do it to whatsisname, don't they?" she shrugged.

"Tom Jones?" Andy suggested.

"Yeah, him!" Cat nodded, pointing a long, orange-painted nail in his direction.

"Listen, give it a rest, will you? All this stuff isn't exactly nice for Kerry to hear!" said Sonja, jokingly wrapping her arm around her friend.

"It's OK," Kerry laughed. "I'm not exactly going to stick a sign around Ollie's neck on stage saying, 'Keep your eyes off my man'! Girls *are* allowed to *look* at him!"

"Just not *touch*," grinned Sonja.

"Exactly," nodded Kerry. "And anyway, I agree with Ollie – I think all that stuff that happened over the weekend was just coincidence."

"But—"

"*But*, Matt," Ollie interrupted his friend, "we all managed to convince ourselves that something was going on with Nick and that escort business.

And *that* was a case of putting two and two together and coming up with sixty-nine..."

"Yeah, maybe you're right," Billy agreed, feeling particularly guilty about his involvement in fuelling that rumour.

The lads all looked over towards the bar where Nick was perched on a stool chatting to the owner of the Railway Tavern as he served pints. Perched next to him was Derek's lovely wife, Eva – once again resplendent in leopard skin and enough make-up to make even Cat shudder. Nick, seeing them gazing at him, tapped his watch.

"We get the hint!" Ollie shouted over, raising up his thumb. "C'mon, boys, time to head backstage and get ready."

"You aren't just being brave about all this, are you?" Anna asked Kerry as soon as the lads had clattered off. "Are you sure all this nonsense with that girl isn't stressing you out?"

"No, I'm fine, honestly!" Kerry insisted. It was sweet, but it irritated her slightly the way everyone had been treating her like she was made of fragile china since the accident. "It's all just a laugh isn't it?"

"Well, good for you. That's the best way to treat it," smiled Anna encouragingly.

Just as long as it doesn't go any further than this, Kerry added silently.

"Well, I still think we should keep an eye on Stalker Girl, and her mate, if they turn up tonight..." growled Cat. "What do you reckon, Maya?"

Maya realised she hadn't said much so far this evening. But to be honest – much as she cared about Ollie – right now, she couldn't care less whether Stalker Girl turned up or not.

There was only one person she hoped might turn up to see the band.

• • •

"Coast seems clear!" Billy grinned at Ollie between numbers. "No sign of SG!"

Ollie knew. He'd been staring out into the audience so much during the last few numbers that he'd forgotten his lyrics twice, and had only saved himself by repeating earlier verses a couple of times. But in all his staring, he had noticed someone he hadn't expected to see.

"Spotted who *is* here?" he said to his guitarist.

"No," said Billy, squinting out into the sea of faces. "Who?"

"That tutor bloke of yours. Must be a fan after coming last week!"

Billy squinted again and could just make out the

tall figure of Alex standing way at the back, by the door.

As Joe counted them in to the next song with his drumsticks, Billy couldn't help but notice that Alex's attention wasn't directed at the stage. He seemed to be staring over to the left – over to where Maya was sitting with the other girls.

CHAPTER 12

●●●●●●●●●●●●●●●●●●●●●●●●●●●●●●

JUST THE TWO OF US...

Maya stood on the chilly station forecourt and looked down at what she was wearing. She'd made too much of an effort, she knew.

Why didn't I just wear my black trousers? she fretted, watching as the gauzy pale sea-green of her new dress – the Lottie cast-off from Sonja's free-for-all rummage a couple of Fridays back – fluttered out like a banner from beneath her long black coat.

The station had been buzzing with Saturday morning shoppers, all heading up to the city for a day out. But so far, there was no sign of anyone else from photography club, and that included Alex.

Maybe I shouldn't have come today. Not while I'm in this stupid mood, Maya thought, noting the hands of the station clock crawl towards 10 o'clock. The train they were meant to catch was at five past. *If I'd given this a miss, and then if I skip a couple of Wednesday night classes, then maybe I'll get things back in perspective. If I just stay away from Alex. Yes, maybe I should just go home – before anyone else arrives...*

"Maya!"

Alex took a second to smile. The expression on his face just the moment before he forced the corners of his mouth upwards was hard for Maya to read. The slight furrow of the brow, the strange look in his eyes... what was running through his mind?

"Hi, Alex!" she said as casually as she could, although she was sure it didn't sound casual.

"Where's everyone else?"

I wish I knew... she thought, feeling her toes curl with embarrassment.

"No sign of anyone. And I've been here quite a while," she shrugged.

Alex said nothing. He glanced first at his watch and then at the departures board, before peering back in the direction of Station Road. The silence felt leaden.

Is it being alone with me that's got him worried? Maya thought fast, scanning his face for clues.

I'm sure he was avoiding me at the club on Wednesday. Did I do something on Saturday night at the party that annoyed him or freaked him out?

She trawled through her memory banks; she'd been pleasant to everyone, even that guy Sam when he was drunkenly coming on to her. The only awkward moment was when her eyes had met Alex's for that split second as they tidied the broken glass; but she'd looked away quickly and started talking about getting a cloth for the red wine that had spilt. Had he even been aware of that look? Or was it something different – had she overstayed her welcome, hanging on for another hour when the other girls from the club had long since gone?

Maybe he just wanted to be with his own friends by then. Maybe... Oh, God— Maya realised in a flash. *What if everyone was thinking like that guy Sam? What if they thought I was just some silly little schoolgirl hanging round her teacher with some pathetic crush? What if Alex thought that too? Maybe he thinks I'm like that Stalker Girl who's been hanging round Ollie...*

The whole idea was seedy and depressing, but it seemed to make sense. What would a teacher do if a pupil was showing signs of falling for him?

Become more distant. To Maya, it *definitely* made sense.

"Well," Alex broke the silence at last, "it looks like it's just you and me, Maya. Shall we get going?"

"Mmm," Maya nodded, wondering which one of them was dreading this more.

• • •

Alex and Maya both stood with their heads tilted so far over to the right that their ears nearly touched their shoulders.

"What do you think of this one?" asked Alex, not taking his eyes off the photo collage in front of them.

"I'm, er, not sure..." Maya muttered, trying to make sense of the confused multiple images.

"Not sure they've hung it up the right way?"

The giggle erupted involuntarily. Maya clapped a hand over her mouth and glanced around quickly in case she offended any earnest art lovers around her.

Alex grinned at her. "And what does *this* one say to you?"

Maya bit her lip and tried really hard to suppress more giggles that were pressing inside her chest.

It was another collage by the same artist and it was more bizarre than the first. In among a jumble of snaps taken in supermarkets was the figure of a housewife pushing a shopping trolley, but with a giant hamburger for a head.

"Um, I guess it's some kind of statement about the consumer society?" she managed, trying to remember that the purpose of this outing was meant to be vaguely educational.

"Really?" Alex nodded, gazing back at the picture, while rubbing his chin thoughtfully. "To me, that hamburger just says... let's get out of this exhibition and find the café. C'mon, I'm starving!"

Maya followed his back with her eyes as he weaved between a viewing public who obviously saw more in the pictures on the walls than either she or Alex did.

What a relief that he thinks this is a load of pompous old rubbish too! she sighed to herself as she slipped through the crowd towards the door. *And what a relief today's turned out all right!*

The train journey up had felt a little frosty at first, but the awkward spell had been broken when Alex started talking and asked about Billy and Andy and the band. Maya had been surprised when Alex mentioned he'd popped in to the

Railway Tavern on Thursday and caught a few numbers of The Loud's set: she hadn't seen him. He'd been on his way somewhere, he'd told her, and hadn't spotted her to say hello, the pub was so busy by that time.

Being able to talk about the band and the boys had made her feel more normal. In fact, she'd felt so relaxed so quickly, it seemed as if the strange spell of the last couple of weeks had been broken. All the tension was gone; all thoughts of tarot readings and predictions left her mind; speaking to Alex felt comfy and normal again.

But it was better than normal. At photography club – with him pottering around everyone in teacher mode – she'd never had the chance to find out how funny Alex really was. She'd seen glimpses of it the first night he'd come to see the band, when he'd joked around and made Cat cackle her embarrassingly dirty laugh, and she'd been aware of it at his flat-warming party too. And on the train this morning, he'd had her crying with laughter as he recounted trying to pour a reluctant and rubber-legged Sam into a taxi at the end of the night, after he'd drunkenly tried to chat up every other girl in the room – even those with boyfriends.

"Well, I'm pretty glad I only made *you* suffer

today!" he exclaimed as they emerged into a quiet gallery corridor outside the exhibition. "I'd never have forgiven myself if I'd dragged everyone from the club along to that load of cobblers!"

"But I felt terrible giggling when everyone else was looking so serious!" Maya admitted, padding along beside Alex as they headed towards the gallery's coffee shop. She had to practically stop herself giving him a playful dig in the stomach for setting her off – it's what she would have automatically done if Matt or Ollie had pulled the same trick.

"Ah, but people can take art *too* seriously. And just 'cause something's hung on a wall, doesn't automatically make it good!" he beamed at her. "Now here..."

He ushered her over to a black and white print on the corridor wall, part of the gallery's permanent collection.

"...to me, this is miles better than that arty junk back there!"

Maya stared at a brooding skyline, rain-filled clouds hanging low and dark over a barren but beautiful American plain.

"It's a bit like your stuff," Maya pointed out, thinking of the blown-up prints on Alex's pale blue walls.

"I guess that's why I like it," he admitted with a wry smile.

"The sky reminds me of your picture on the mantelpiece, the one that got broken."

"Ah, yeah – the one of Charlotte."

Maya felt a jolt shake her out of her good mood. "Who?"

"Charlotte, my girlfriend. Took that one when we were on holiday in Greece one year."

After forgetting herself to the point that she felt like she was hanging out with a friend for the afternoon, Maya suddenly felt like the silly little school kid all over again.

CHAPTER 13

. . . .

SENSE AND SENSIBILITY

Maya closed the magazine that she wasn't reading and took another sip of coffee from the Styrofoam cup.

"...an' *she* says, 'Don't you *know* how I feel about you?', an' *he* says, 'Don't say anything, I don't want to hear it.'"

"Did he?"

Somehow, Maya couldn't help listening in to the conversation of the two young mums sitting next to her at the booth by the lake. Over in the distance, their children were tearing about with Ravi and the other kids on the swings and climbing frames of the playpark.

"Yeah, he did. An' then she says to him, 'But you've *got* to hear it! I'm crazy about you! I can't stop thinking about you!'"

"Nah!"

"Yeah! An' then he says, 'But you know I can't be with you – you *know* I'm with someone else...'"

Maya gave a little shudder and it wasn't just because the wintry sunshine this Sunday afternoon was too weak to warm the chilly air. Whoever the women were talking about – it struck a chord in her, whether she wanted it to or not.

"What happened then?"

"Dunno. The phone rang, so I missed it. S'pose we'll just have to watch tomorrow night's episode and see if we can pick it up from there."

Smiling to herself, it suddenly dawned on Maya that she hadn't been listening in to a saga of someone's personal life at all; it was just the latest storyline in *EastEnders*.

A small figure in the distance distracted her; Ravi was leaving his playmates behind and running over to her at the speed of small boy light.

"Maya!" he panted as he came close.

"What?" she asked with concern.

The two mums had stopped their soap catch-up – it was their turn to listen in.

"Jack..." panted Ravi.

"Who's Jack?" she asked. Maya knew most of her little brother's regular playmates, but then every time they came to the park he seemed to hook up with someone new.

"Him!" said Ravi, turning and pointing uselessly at a distant playpark heaving with children.

"What about Jack? What's wrong?"

"He... he..." gasped Ravi, exhausted from his sprint. "He said he'd give me one of his Skips."

"*And...*" prompted Maya, relaxing now that she knew that the emergency wasn't to do with anything more life-threatening than crisps.

"*And* then I took one," explained Ravi, his brown eyes wide. "But I was on the roundabout – and I spilled the whole bag! By accident!"

"So... you want to get him another bag of Skips to make it up?" she guessed.

"Uh-huh," Ravi nodded solemnly.

As Maya searched around in her pockets for some small change, she took comfort in the fact that this was the real world; the world of looking out for little brothers who loved you because you could sort out their crisp crises.

Not some fantasy world where you persuade yourself that you're in love with someone you don't even know properly, and don't have any right to be in love with... she told herself off.

The emotional rollercoaster Maya had suddenly found herself on was driving her crazy. Having her mood swing up to the clouds and back down to a pit of gloom wasn't something Maya was enjoying one little bit. The fact that after the fun she'd had with Alex on the train journey up to the city the day before and all through the exhibition, she'd managed to slip back into some ridiculous ditch of doom after he'd mentioned his girlfriend, irritated her to the point of desperation.

And it all started with that tarot reading! she sighed to herself as she watched Ravi go up to the kiosk with his money. *I wish someone could make sense of this, because I can't.*

But then it suddenly occurred to her – as the women beside her started discussing the latest heart-rending break-up in *Home and Away* – who the very person was who could help her.

• • •

"Could I have some lemonade in that?"

The orange juice was only half-way up the tall glass, so Anna stopped pouring from the carton and squinted in the fridge to see if she had any left.

"OK," she said, spying a quarter full plastic bottle and pulling it out. "There you go, Ravi!"

"Sorry…" Maya apologised as her little brother trotted off to the sofa in Anna's living room, sipping his fizzing drink, while at the same time trying not to drop the bag of crisps or the comic he had tucked under his arm.

"What for?" asked Anna, pouring out the Earl Grey tea she'd made for herself and Maya in her cracked earthenware pot.

"Sorry for bringing him round," Maya nodded towards her brother, who was now transfixed by the explosions in an old James Bond re-run on the telly. "And sorry he's being so demanding – he wouldn't try it on at home."

"A bit of lemonade? Who cares?" Anna smiled, tucking her long, mid-brown hair behind her ears.

"And… sorry for turning up like this," Maya apologised again. "You've only just finished your shift downstairs. You must be exhausted."

"I *am* tired, but just tired of whiny customers – not tired of friends," Anna reassured her. "So is this just a social call or…?"

As Anna trailed off, Maya realised that her confused state of mind must be written across her face.

"I– I–" she tried to begin, casting a quick glance over to her brother to check he wasn't listening in. But with the quadruple delights of Wotsits, orangey lemonade, a comic and an on-screen succession of explosions, there wasn't much chance of that.

Anna smiled at her patiently and pushed Maya's newly-poured cup of Earl Grey across the small table to her.

"It's just that I've been feeling really... *muddled* ever since that tarot reading," Maya explained, although 'muddled' felt like the understatement of the year.

"Did it upset you?" asked Anna, sounding suddenly worried – and possibly guilty, Maya thought, since she'd arranged the day out for the girls to the Psychic Fair.

"No – not *upset*, more unsettled. I mean, it was all so accurate – about my past and my life and everything – but all this stuff about love and life changes..."

"Maya, you know I'm interested in all kinds of New Age stuff, but it doesn't mean I take everything as gospel," said Anna.

Maya immediately thought of Alex and what he'd said about not all art being great just because it was stuck in a gallery. Alex – now there was the real problem.

"I just thought getting our fortunes told was a bit of fun, that's all," Anna continued.

"Listen, Anna, I know you won't say anything to anyone..." Maya began nervously.

"Of course not," the other girl nodded.

"But there's someone I think– I think I've fallen for... and it's stupid, and he doesn't know. And even if he did, he wouldn't – couldn't – feel the same way back..."

Maya wasn't sure she was making any sense, but it felt good to talk to someone about it. Someone like Anna, who wouldn't try and prise out of her – like Sonja or the others might – just *who* exactly she was talking about.

"And you think this is what your fortune foretold?" Anna prompted her.

"Well, no – that's the problem. I think that tarot thing put all this into my head. I don't think I'd have even thought about this... this... *person*," Maya managed to say, though the word 'man' had been the first word on her tongue, "if that tarot-reader hadn't suggested it."

"Well," said Anna measuredly, aware that Maya didn't want to disclose who was really on her mind. "The thing about tarot or any other kind of reading is that it isn't set in stone."

"What do you mean?" asked Maya.

"The tarot-reader just tells you about the path you seem to be on at that moment. But you can change that path at any point and then, of course, your future changes too."

"I don't understand..." said Maya, trying to get her logical mind to make sense of what her friend was telling her.

"It's like... well..." Anna racked her brain for an example. "It's like if someone was in a bad relationship with a boy, a psychic might say that – looking ahead – your love-life was really rocky. But you might decide after that to finish with him completely. And once you've done that, your whole future changes; it's like that reading suddenly becomes invalid. Does that make any sense?"

Maya had a funny feeling that Anna had just told her a true story.

"I think so," she wrinkled up her nose. "So, even if this woman was for real, and genuinely saw love coming up for me..."

"You don't have to follow that path," finished Anna. "If this... *person*... isn't right for you, for whatever reason, then you don't have to go any further with it, or think fate is *throwing* you together for ever. *You* choose."

Maya wasn't sure if that made her feel any better or not. Knowing she didn't have to believe in her tarot reading completely was a relief... but maybe a bit of a disappointment too.

"And don't forget, the rest of us had rubbish readings that day, so who's to say yours wasn't all rubbish too?"

Because everything else that woman in the cardie told me was so accurate, Maya thought to herself, knowing full well that Anna knew that too and was only trying to make her feel better.

"So... this person," Anna smiled gently, running her finger around the rim of her tea cup. "It definitely couldn't happen?"

Maya pictured Alex's grey-blue eyes laughing at her as he joked in the gallery the day before. Then she pictured two more important things: the ten-year age gap between them and that smiling girl on the stormy hillside in the broken frame.

"It *definitely* couldn't happen," Maya croaked, taken aback by the hard knot of what felt like tears and disappointment that had formed in her throat.

CHAPTER 14

●●●●●●●●●●●●●●●●●●●●●●●●●●●●

A TRICKY CUSTOMER

"So how come you've never been to see us play at the Railway Tavern yet?"

"Dunno. Stuff to do, people to see, I s'pose."

Ollie doubted it. Bryan wasn't exactly Mr Gregarious. He wasn't known for his razor-sharp wit and sparkling social skills.

"Anything interesting in there?" Ollie asked, giving up on cross-examining Bryan about his no-show at The Loud's gigs and trying instead to get a conversation going about whatever was so riveting in the *NME* this week.

"Nothin' really..." droned Bryan, never lifting his gaze from the music paper he had spread open on the counter.

Ollie sighed, leaned his weight on the till and stared off towards the window of Nick's Slick Riffs.

There was no point trying to peer out into the street to see if any customers were approaching; the windows were too badly in need of a wash.

Nick tried to keep the café next door scrupulously clean, but he seemed to think a bit of dust and dirt added a certain ambience to the record shop. And on this particular occasion, the daylight was also obscured by huge sale signs, designed to catch the eye of any passing commuters and customers of the End.

Only it was 5.00 pm this Monday afternoon and it couldn't really be said that the sale signs had done their job. The usual mixed handful of regulars had bumbled in, trawled the racks of second-hand records and CDs, and bumbled back out again. It was just the laid-back level of non-business that suited Bryan down to the ground, but for Ollie – used to tearing around a busy café and kitchen juggling orders and charming customers left, right and centre – it wasn't exactly fascinating work.

He didn't mind working in the record shop when Bryan was off on holiday or skiving off with Nick buying stock. *Then* Slick Riffs became Ollie's playground – he could indulge in listening to whatever music he wanted to at practically whatever volume he fancied, while serving the odd music enthusiast who happened by. But being seconded to 'help Bryan out' during a sale frenzy that had never happened (and, obviously, was never *going* to happen) was enough to numb his brain.

"I thought Nick would have been twisting your arm to come along to see us since he's our manager?" Ollie tried again to make conversation. He knew Bryan and Nick were long-time drinking buddies, sharing a passion (well hidden in Bryan's case) for old rock music.

"Nope..." droned Bryan, flipping a page over.

"You normally head over to the Railway Tavern for a pint after work most nights with Nick, don't you?"

"Uh-huh."

"So why don't you just hang around one Thursday night and check us out?"

"Mmm," grunted Bryan. "Might do."

"We do a lot of numbers I'm sure you'd be into," Ollie persisted, staring at the top of Bryan's shaggy head of hair bent over the *NME*'s reviews section.

"Mmmm..."

It didn't seem as if Bryan was paying a whole lot of attention. Ollie decided to try a new tack.

"Yeah, all our songs are based on ancient Tibetan monk chants."

"Uh-huh."

"We come on stage in gold lurex jumpsuits."

"Right."

"And Joe plays drums with a snake draped round his neck."

"Uh-huh."

"And we've got these girls who come on if we get an encore and they belly dance across the stage."

"Mmmm..."

Ollie was starting to enjoy himself now. Talking rubbish to Bryan till he noticed could help pass the time quite nicely.

"And then when everyone's clapping at the end, we release these cages of wild flamingos."

"Uh-huh."

"And—"

Suddenly the door rattled open and, with the imminent arrival of a potential purchaser, the two salesmen sprang into action: Ollie leaping to a standing position behind the counter instead of leaning laconically over the till; Bryan raising his sleepy eyes from the printed page to observe the doorway.

"Hello..." she said, almost shyly, as she walked towards the counter.

"Uh, huh– hi," Ollie stuttered, feeling himself

twitch with surprise at the sight of Stalker Girl. He'd completely forgotten about her – been relieved to forget about her – since her non-appearance at the gig on Thursday. She hadn't been in the End for a week, the teasing (courtesy of Matt and Catrina) seemed to have died down, and he'd thought – hoped – that was it.

Wrong! thought Ollie, wondering what was going to come next.

Stalker Girl lowered her head coquettishly and began twirling one finger through a strand of her dark fringe. Her gaze was for Ollie only as if Bryan was totally invisible.

Sensing this, Bryan relaxed and carried on reading his music paper.

"Can I, um, help?" said Ollie, trying to sound matter-of-fact.

If she's here to tell me she did *send that picture on Valentine's Day or that it* was *her who left that weird message at the caff last weekend, I'm going to throw up*, thought Ollie, feeling prickles of cold, panicky sweat break out on his skin.

"Your friend next door, the waitress girl, told me you were here..." said Stalker Girl in a tiny, baby-doll voice.

Thanks a lot, Anna, Ollie grumbled silently as he studied SG's face and tried to work out how old she was. Not as young as that voice, though, that was for sure.

"Uh-huh," he muttered non-committally.

Maybe about fifteen, Ollie decided silently.

"So..." said Stalker Girl, twirling from side to side, glancing at the racks that lined both walls of the shop. "Got any of your own CDs in here?"

Ollie looked at her quizzically. It took a second for him to realise that she meant The Loud, not his own music collection at home.

Bryan snorted, but didn't look up.

"Well, The Loud aren't really at that stage yet," Ollie shrugged. "Hopefully, if we get spotted by a record company, we might, uh..."

His words fizzled out and he finished his sentence with another shrug instead.

"Listen, I just wanted to..." the girl began, then paused.

A gulp in Ollie's throat seemed wedged midway between going up or going down as he waited to hear what she was about to come out with.

"I just wanted to say sorry," she said, lifting her hands on to the counter and drumming her fingers agitatedly on its surface.

Stalker Girl was getting way too close for comfort.

Moving his hands off the other side of the counter, Ollie knew it was his turn to speak.

"Sorry for what?" his voice came out in a squeak as he scanned her pale, slight face for clues to what was on her mind.

"Sorry for missing the gig on Thursday night," she explained. "I've had flu."

"That's, uh, OK," Ollie grunted, momentarily distracted with thoughts of what Matt would make of this bizarre little encounter. ("What, so all the regulars of the Railway Tavern have to come in with a note from their mummy if they miss a Thursday night? I tell you, Ol, that is one *weird* girl...")

"But I didn't want to miss it – I love coming to see you... uh, your band," said the girl, now leaning her elbows on the counter.

"Well, that's nice..." Ollie waffled, taking a step back and wishing Bryan had a bit more savvy and could see that he needed help.

"Astrid," said the dark-haired girl, thinking Ollie's hesitation was down to him being unsure of her name.

"Er, Ollie," Ollie offered a reluctant introduction.

"I know..."

She was staring at him again and he didn't know what he was meant to say or do.

"Yeah, Thursday night... it was really busy. So, no problem," he mumbled and followed it with a strangled attempt at a laugh.

"But I just wanted to be there, to cheer you on..." she gazed up at him with adoring, unblinking dark eyes.

"Well, all our mates were there doing that. Y'know, Kerry and the other girls."

Ollie didn't know if she knew Kerry and everyone, but it suddenly struck him that it might be a good idea to drop his girlfriend's name into the conversation.

"Those girls..." said Astrid, with a little twitch at the side of her mouth, "the waitress and the others. They're all just your friends?"

"Yeah. Well, no," Ollie shuffled on his side of the counter. "I go out with Kerry."

"Kerry...?"

The girl's eyes widened so much at her name that Ollie immediately thought of the exaggerated eyes of every Disney heroine ever.

"Um, Kerry – with the longish curly hair?" he awkwardly explained, waving his hands stupidly around his head.

"But... but I thought she was just..."

The dark-haired girl had pushed herself up to a standing position and was now clenching both her hands under her chin, her eyes darting about all over the place.

"A mate?" suggested Ollie. "No, we've been going out together for ages."

He felt pleased with himself; the mention of Kerry seemed to have hit home with Astrid somehow. Maybe now she would just back off and leave him alone a little more; be a little more normal...

His heart sank as his eyes met hers; now even more Disneyesque as they filled with huge, fat tears.

"Listen, I'm sorry, uh, Astrid," Ollie scrambled for words.

"You– you–" she stammered, struggling for a suitably damning word. "How could you?"

Ollie shrugged helplessly as the girl turned and ran out of the shop.

The dust floated in the silent air as the reverberation of the slamming shop door rattled round Ollie's stunned head.

"Hur-hur... Just like Mick..."

Ollie shot a glance round at Bryan, who was chuckling away to himself.

"What?" Ollie asked, feeling as weak and wobbly as if he'd just done ten rounds with Prince Naseem.

"You're just like Mick Jagger – always breaking the hearts of all the girl fans!" Bryan guffawed, laddishly amused.

Ollie suddenly wondered if a future career as a Vespa repair man wasn't safer than the route he'd chosen.

CHAPTER 15

● ●

FREEZE FRAME

Outside the breeze-block hut, flakes of white snow whirled in the dark night air.

The weather, plus the wave of flu that had hit the town's population, had affected the turn-out tonight. There weren't that many people at the photography club, and – unusually – Maya found she had the dark room all to herself.

Hope it stays this way, she mused as she set up the developing trays. Being on her own suited her at the moment – having the bustle of people around her only made her thoughts more jumbled and incoherent.

It wouldn't have been so bad if she could talk over her state of mind with one of her friends, but she didn't want to bother Anna again – and after running through the roll call of the rest, she decided it was a bad idea to consult any of them.

To fall for someone who was practically a teacher was totally taboo – her mates would put it different ways, but they'd all be scandalised and eventually suggest that it would be a good move to drop the idea and drop out of the club, she was sure. Well, all except Cat, who'd find the whole thing deliciously shocking, tell her to go for it and then revel in gossiping about it.

Neither option suited Maya. The very idea of giving up photography – and giving up the chance to see Alex every week – filled her with misery. But then again, the very idea of anything happening between them was unsettling to say the least, as well as impossible. Considering that Alex didn't think of Maya in any way except as one of the many people he taught – not forgetting the matter of his girlfriend – the chances of anything developing between them was a whole lot *less* than zero.

Developing between us... Maya repeated in her head, aware of the terrible photography pun she'd just made.

Walking over to the door, she flicked two switches simultaneously, swapping harsh, overhead fluorescent lighting for an amniotic, soft red glow.

It's not like I can talk to anyone about how I feel anyway — considering I don't really know how I feel myself, she agonised, flopping down on a tall stool by the work surface.

Staring blankly at the film spool in her hand, Maya decided that if she couldn't trust a friend to analyse the mad train of thoughts jostling for space in her head, there was only one person who could help.

Herself.

Maya, when did you first realise you liked Alex?

From Day One, she answered her cross-examining self. *When I first joined the club. He was so friendly and easy to talk to. Not like any teachers I'd ever met.*

Did you feel something stronger than just 'liking' way back then?

No — I don't think so.

When did it change for you then?

I guess it was that moment at the party, when our fingers touched.

What happened?

I felt like my whole body had had an electric shock — as if what started as a tingle when my skin brushed against his shot all the way through me, and made my heart lurch.

Ouch! So, is that the definition of love? An electric shock?

Sounds stupid, I know. And it can't just be that – it's like that corny idea of cupid shooting his arrow, and I don't buy that.

Is that what's bothering you? That you don't believe in that instantaneous, love-at-first sight kind of thing?

Yes, I suppose so. I just don't think it's possible.

But it wasn't love at first sight, was it? her analytical side pointed out. *You've got to know Alex gradually over the months, been inspired by him, had a laugh with him, got to see what a nice guy he is...*

So what are you trying to say? argued the muddled side of Maya. *I mean, I meet nice people I can have a laugh with all the time – and I don't manage to persuade myself I'm in love with them.*

Ah, but I think you've been slowly falling for Alex for a long time... you've just never admitted it to yourself. It took that one moment at the party to make the whole thing obvious.

The muddled Maya sat quietly in the rosy glow of the room, absorbing that thought. It felt true, it felt right. But somehow, it didn't make her feel any better.

So, say that I am in love with him – where does that get me? It's still never going to happen. Not with the job he does, not with the fact that he has a girlfriend, not with the age difference, not with the fact that my parents would totally flip out at the very idea, and apart from anything, he doesn't even remotely fancy me!

Hey, said the calmer side of her. *Here's the deal: you're allowed to love someone – but they're under no obligation to love you back...*

And that's supposed to make me feel better?

Yes – and I think it will. If you just stop doing a Kerry, and worrying yourself to pieces, and just accept things are the way they are, then you'll be fine.

Will I?

Yes. Trust me. Trust yourself...

Maybe it was her personal heart-to-heart, and maybe it was the soothing red glow of the darkroom lamp, but Maya was aware of how relaxed she suddenly felt.

Until the sharp knock at the door.

"It's OK, you can come in!" she called out, cursing the fact that one of the others had decided to join her. She hoped it wasn't Ashleigh or Jane; she wasn't in the mood for their endless chitter-chatter tonight.

"Sorry, Maya – I just need to grab something out of the drawer," Alex apologised, a harsh shard of bright light shining behind him.

The Scottish burr of his deep voice sounded gruff and warm at the same time.

"It's– it's, um, OK," Maya stumbled over her words. She didn't believe in mind-reading, but couldn't stop herself praying that he wouldn't be able to sense what had just been running through her head.

Alex stepped into the room, closing the door behind him and plunging them both into the red-tinged gloom.

"Sorry," he repeated as he moved hazily towards her.

Sorry for what? she flustered, then realised he was trying to get to the drawer directly behind her.

"Oh, right – I'll move," mumbled Maya, slipping off the stool.

"No, you're all right, I can reach from here..."

Maya tried to step out of his way, but instead, found herself right in it. She felt herself collide with his chest.

It was a moment for "oops!" and apologies and awkward laughter as they sprang apart, but somehow, that didn't happen.

Instead, Maya felt herself freeze-framed, her hands spread out on the wiry muscles of his arms, her eyes drawn in the red dusk to the triangle of smooth skin showing at the unbuttoned neck of his shirt, just a breath away from her. Not that she could breathe; her lungs were temporarily paralysed, caught in the unexpectedness of the moment.

Then everything began to move in slow rose-tinted motion... Maya tilted her head up and looked into his troubled, searching eyes.

He wasn't breathing either, she realised.

Trembling slightly, Maya stretched up on her tiptoes, then felt him lean down towards her.

Their kiss was soft and tentative as if neither dared believe it was really happening...

The sudden hammering at the dark room door was real enough, though – so was the clattering of the stool, as they broke away from each other and sent it spinning to the floor.

CHAPTER 16

• •

DOUBLE TROUBLE

"That's it – it's all over!"

Cat slapped her hand down emphatically on the pub table.

"I know I don't say this very often," said Sonja, looking straight at Kerry as she talked, "but Cat's right. That's the end of Stalker Girl."

"It's like all the boy bands – they keep quiet about having girlfriends and wives and forty-two children in case it puts any fans off."

Kerry nodded at Cat's words. She knew what she meant; when that Astrid girl had found out that Ollie had a girlfriend, it would surely have burst whatever romantic bubble she had in her head.

"Just the way she started crying when she was talking to Ollie says it all. Stalker Girl obviously had this big delusion about going out with a pop star—"

"—or at least some bloke in a pub band," Cat corrected her cousin with a snigger.

"Yeah, yeah, whatever," Sonja tried to continue, shooting a sideways glance at Cat. "So she has this delusion about going out with the closest thing Winstead's got to a pop star—"

"Ollie," nodded Kerry. She knew this was all for her benefit. The girls – and Ollie – had been trying to reassure her about the strange little encounter in the record shop all week.

"Yeah, Ollie," agreed Sonja. "And now that she knows she can't have him, she won't show her face round here again."

"It's funny that she didn't realise you two were together," Anna pointed out, twirling a beer mat round with her finger on the sticky table. "If Joe's right and she's been coming practically every Thursday since The Loud started playing here, she must have seen the way you two are with each other."

"Yes, but remember what Ollie's like," Maya chipped in. "He's always fooling around with all of us. If you were just watching from a distance, you might not realise that when he puts an arm round Kerry, it's any different from when – for example – you and him start larking about, Son."

The girls all shrugged and nodded. It was true; Ollie mucked about like a brother with them and was very relaxed and tactile, just like a girl mate would be.

Glancing over, Maya spotted the resigned smile on Kerry's face. Her friend might be fed up with the constant discussion about the weird Stalker Girl, but Maya was really glad of it. Because of what had happened, she was sure her face gave her away; sure it had 'guilty' written all over it.

Brigid, who looked after the junior Joshis till their parents got home form work, had already asked if Maya was all right. And while she'd tried to assure the understanding Irish woman that nothing was troubling her, she'd felt Sunny's eyes boring into her. Alerted by Brigid's concern, Sunny had started scanning her older sister for clues, searching for weaknesses she could store up and use against her in the future.

Maya knew it sounded ridiculous to be so wary of her younger sister, but Sunny had told tales on Maya enough times before for Maya to know to be on her guard.

"Well, let's forget about that stupid girl and have a good time tonight. I'm going to get some more drinks before the lads come on," said Sonja, standing up. "Do you want to give me a hand, Maya?"

Maya nodded and followed Sonja over to the less crowded end of the bar.

"Maybe we should move up a bit," Maya pointed out, nodding up towards the huddle of people waiting to be served by the two men darting about between the pumps and the till. "I don't think Derek or that other barman will see us to serve us here."

"They'll spot us eventually," said Sonja, tossing her blonde hair back and leaning on the bar top.

Of course they will, Maya laughed to herself, watching several pairs of male eyes swivel round and glue themselves to her friend.

"Actually, I just wanted to have a quick word away from everyone..."

Maya's heart sank. What was this going to be about?

"You've been really quiet the last couple of weeks or so, Maya, and – don't take this the wrong way or anything – but you don't exactly look great at the moment. Are you OK?"

Maya knew what Sonja was saying was true; she'd tried to cover up the dark shadows under eyes with concealer, but it was hard to find a good match for her skin tone. Maybe if she hadn't lain awake all night, going over and over what had happened in the dark room, her skin wouldn't be telling tales on her.

"Yes, I'm fine – just starting to get my head round a lot of studying right now," Maya lied.

"Your parents aren't hassling you again, are they?" Sonja asked with concern. It had taken a lot of effort on Maya's part to win a little more freedom from her mother and father and they were still keen on drumming home the message that hard work was more important than fun to their children.

"No, no, they're not too bad."

Sonja didn't look convinced.

"Billy's worried about you too," she announced, sending Maya's heart lurching into her throat.

It had been Billy who'd walked in on her and Alex the night before. As he'd peered around the door, Alex busied himself with picking up the stool from the floor; but Maya had felt herself stand wobbling rootlessly, her arms wrapped shyly around herself, with God knows what expression slapped on her face.

Maya raised her eyebrows questioningly at Sonja, not trusting herself to speak.

"I was talking to Billy before you arrived tonight and he told me that you had to leave your photography club early yesterday 'cause you didn't feel well. He says you looked like you were shivering or shaking or something."

"I'd had a headache all day," Maya shrugged. "Being in the dark room just made it worse, that was all. It's gone now."

"You know something...?"

Maya was relieved to see a tiny knowing smile spread across her friend's face.

"What?" she replied.

"Billy really cares about you. Y'know, like *really* cares about you."

Maya rolled her eyes to the ceiling: she suspected she'd been discussed in more detail than she'd have liked.

"I know this is none of my business, Maya, and I don't want to sound pushy like Cat," Sonja smiled nervously, "but you could do a lot worse than Billy and he's told me before that he's crazy about you."

Her suspicions were confirmed. Billy *had* been gently flirting with her recently and all because he'd heard about her dumb tarot reading from someone in her crowd.

"Did he send me that Valentine card?" Maya asked point-blank.

"*Welllllll...*" squirmed Sonja.

"In other words, yes. C'mon, Son – you're spilling the poor lad's secrets here, so you might as well spill that one."

"Don't sound so annoyed, Maya!" said Sonja, looking hurt. "I only thought you'd be flattered.

He said he was thinking of sending you a card and I told him to go for it."

Sonja hated to be compared to her cousin, but sometimes – more than she could ever see herself – they were very alike. And subtlety, for both girls, was *not* always high on their agenda.

"Look, I like Billy a lot," Maya sighed, "but not in *that* way. And the last thing I need is my friends encouraging him to think I might fancy him, OK?"

"OK! I didn't mean to—"

The apology was wasted. At that moment, Maya's panicked eyes were fixed on a point over Sonja's shoulder.

Turning around, Sonja found herself looking up into the gaunt face of Maya's tutor. The black shadows under his eyes, she noticed, were nearly a match for Maya's.

"Maya – I've got to talk to you!" Alex blurted out as if Sonja, standing between them, was invisible.

• • •

"What was all that about?" asked Cat, her mascara-heavy eyes wide with curiosity.

"I don't know – he wanted to speak to her and they went out. That was it."

Anna, Cat and Kerry stared intently at Sonja,

desperate for information. She only wished she could give them some.

"But what did he say exactly?" asked Kerry.

"He said he had to talk to her."

"And what did Maya say?" questioned Cat.

"She didn't say anything – she just followed him out," Sonja explained as best she could. It didn't make sense to her either.

"Maybe there's a problem with the photography club," suggested Anna, although in the back of her mind she was recalling the conversation they'd had when Maya had stopped by her flat. When she'd mentioned a certain unnamed person...

"Yeah, maybe the whole building burned down!" gasped Cat in her usual overboard manner.

"Shut up, Cat. Anyhow, it's probably something to do with her being ill last night," Sonja reasoned. "Alex probably just wanted to check she's all right."

"Of course," nodded Kerry. Although like all the girls, she found it hard to believe. A teacher tracking you down just to check on your health?

Ollie's voice booming down the mike interrupted their speculations.

"Hi, everyone! We're The Loud!"

Sonja watched Kerry's face automatically break

into a smile. She knew how she was feeling. All the girls felt a mixture of pride, excitement and nervousness as they watched their boys step on stage. But Kerry, of course, had love bundled into the whole mixture as well.

Then a shadow fell over their table. The lights of the stage were eclipsed by a slim black cloud...

"Bitch!" hissed Astrid, practically spitting her venom and spoilt hopes on to a startled Kerry.

In a second she was gone, lost in the shuffling, anticipant crowd.

It might have seemed like a bad dream, if the very real tears of shock and hurt weren't spilling down Kerry's freckled cheeks.

CHAPTER 17

• •

COLD COMFORT

"I'm sorry – I shouldn't have..."

"Shouldn't have what?" asked Maya, shivering in the cold night air. She wished she'd grabbed her coat before following Alex out of the pub and into the station car park.

"Last night – I shouldn't have kissed you!" Alex burst out, looking totally traumatised.

"Actually, I think it was me that kissed you," Maya pointed out.

"But we shouldn't have done it!"

"It was a kiss, Alex, that was all. We didn't run off to Las Vegas and get married or anything!"

Seeing the stress written over Alex's face brought out Maya's natural instinct to bring calm and good sense to a situation. Her own anxieties slipped away as she tried to soothe him.

"How can you make jokes?" he said, holding his long arms out at his sides. "This is serious stuff! I couldn't sleep last night for turning the whole thing over in my head..."

"I wasn't making a joke," Maya tried to explain. "I was just pointing out that—"

"You must have thought it was serious too or you wouldn't have left like that..."

The glow of the yellow street lamp directly above them exaggerated the gauntness of Alex's face, making him look like some heartbreakingly sad, undernourished stray dog on *Animal Hospital*.

More than anything, Maya wanted to grab him in her arms and tell him everything would be all right.

"I left because I felt... confused," she explained, resisting the impulse to hug him.

"And now?"

Maya bit her lip, her false confidence suddenly ebbing away.

"I don't know exactly," she trembled, holding her arms tightly across her chest. "All I *do* know is that when I saw your face in there just now, I was... I was *so* happy."

"Oh, Maya," groaned Alex. "C'mere..."

Without hesitating, she stepped forward into his embrace. Her hands slipped inside his fleece-lined jacket, wrapping themselves tightly around his waist. She turned her head slightly and laid it against his chest, her eyes tight closed.

Alex pulled his jacket around her protectively, hugging her close to him in the biting wind.

"I'm your teacher – this isn't right..." his voice came from above her as he rested his chin on the top of her head.

"But you're not *my* teacher," Maya replied, her voice muffled beneath the jacket. She'd never felt so warm and cared for before. She felt she could stay there, snuggled together, listening to his heartbeat, for ever.

"But—"

"But nothing," she mumbled happily. "You're a lecturer at an Adult Education Centre and I'm an adult. It's not like some seedy teacher-pupil thing."

"I suppose..."

Maya's idyll had lasted for all of thirty seconds when a terrible thought occurred to her. A terrible thought that involved a picture in a broken frame.

"Alex...?" she whispered, now squeezing her eyes tight shut against the question she was about to ask and the answer she didn't want to hear.

"Uh-huh?"

"What about Charlotte?"

"Charlotte?" said Alex with surprise. He pulled back slightly and looked down into Maya's face.

She gazed back up at him and waited to hear the worst.

"Maya, Charlotte was years ago. We went out together at university."

"But you've still got her picture..."

"'Course! She's a great girl and still a mate. I stayed with her and her husband when I was in Edinburgh for the Festival last year. Her wee boy calls me Uncle Alex!"

Muddled among her feelings of relief, a small niggle of doubt troubled her. It was a sense of being out of her depth: Maya had never had a boyfriend before, only ever had one date – with Billy – and now here she was, on the verge of... *something* with a man whose friends were old enough to be married with children. It felt a long way from meeting up with her mates after school in the End-of-the-Line café, gossiping over Cat's latest skirt length and deciding which type of doughnut to go for.

"Did you think she was still around?" he said softly, his grey-blue eyes crinkling at the corners as he smiled.

"Well, yes," she nodded back up at him.

The stared at each other for a second, lost in happiness and confusion.

"What are we going to do, Maya?"

"I don't know," she smiled up at Alex, slipping her arms from around his waist and placing her hands on either side of his face.

Slowly, she drew him down to kiss her.

CHAPTER 18

• •

DOUBLE TAKE

"Barney – stop pulling!"

It was obvious to Kerry what was gripping her dog's attention to the point of strangling himself on his collar: up ahead was a red setter they often saw being walked in the park. Unfortunately, Barney had too few brain cells to figure out that when the red setter bared its teeth and growled at him, it was a sign of deep loathing rather than any indication that it wanted to play.

"Sit down, Barney," Kerry urged the dog, pushing his reluctant bottom downwards "Let's wait here a minute until that stupid dog's out of sight."

Barney thought better of resisting and parked himself on the pavement, his tongue lolling to one side of his mouth and his doggy gaze fixed on the receding form of the setter.

Kerry leaned on the edge of the bridge and caught her breath. She loved her dog and adored her little brother – she was on her way to pick him up from a friend's house – but they both forgot that they were meant to play 'nicely' with her till her cracked bones had properly healed.

Being a dog, Barney had an excuse for constantly overstepping the mark, but Lewis – at seven – should have known better. Only this morning, he'd dive-bombed her in bed, desperate to show her the small plastic blob he'd got free in his box of cereal.

"D'you like it?" he'd yelped, before realising that his big sister couldn't talk for the pain he'd inflicted by landing a direct hit on her ribs.

He'd tried to make it up to her by selflessly giving her the plastic blob as a get well gift. She found it sitting on her spoon when she finally made it down for breakfast.

"It's for you, apparently," her mum had explained when she saw Kerry peering short-sightedly at it. "Lewis said it was your turn to get the toy. Very generous of him, don't you think?" she'd said, smiling.

Kerry put her hand in her jacket pocket and let her fingers curl around the unidentifiable lump of freebie plastic. A kids' thing really. Still, it was nice to feel loved – even by an overenthusiastic little brother – after last night.

Ignoring the roar and bright headlights of the Friday evening traffic moving past her, Kerry leaned over and looked down at the Guinness-black river, its occasional ripples catching the light from the old-fashioned lamps along the path.

How could she do that? Kerry wondered, replaying the incident again in her head. *How could that girl just walk up to someone she didn't know and call them a bitch?*

Poor Ollie had been frantic when they came off stage – he hadn't even known what had gone on as he introduced the band. With the glare of the spotlights, the sea of faces and the fact that it had all happened in a flash, Kerry knew that he and the boys were oblivious to the Stalker Girl incident. Even though the tears of injustice were still coursing down her cheeks, Kerry had been adamant that she was fine and begged the others not to cause a fuss or any kind of commotion that might alert anyone in the band to what had happened.

Reluctantly, she'd agreed that Cat should nip off and check that Stalker Girl had left the pub, and was relieved when it was confirmed that she had. Cat came back in with Maya, who'd seen Stalker Girl run off crying into the night while she was outside talking to Alex, and suddenly everyone's attention had turned to her.

"Alex was just passing and thought he'd see if I was here – see if I was all right after feeling ill last night," Maya had lied to her friends, wide-eyed.

Kerry had managed to dry her eyes by this time. She nodded and tried to look interested, all the time willing her lip to stop trembling and the tears not to start again.

They did, of course, as soon as Sonja gabbled out the story to Ollie later and he went to give her a comforting hug.

"I– I– I'm oh– OK," she'd hiccuped as the other boys ambled over and were shocked to hear what had happened.

"Told you she was weird!" Matt had announced. "Didn't I say that right from the start?"

"Yeah, you did," Ollie agreed, his face dark with anger one second, the next crumpling with sympathy and guilt when he looked into Kerry's watery eyes.

"But I think that it's definitely all over now, don't you?" suggested Joe.

"Why?" asked Billy, scratching his head.

"'Cause Stalker Girl didn't stick around to see the band, did she?" Cat joined in. "The mad cow finds out Ollie's got a girlfriend, gets her jealousy off her chest by yelling at that girlfriend, and then disappears off into the night, never to be seen again. Finito."

"Yeah," nodded Sonja. "Like they say on *Friends*, that's 'closure'."

"I hope so," Ollie had said, giving Kerry a squeeze. "'Cause if she comes near Kerry or me again I don't know what I'll do..."

Looking over now into the dark waters of the river, Kerry smiled at her knight in shining armour's words – it was almost worth being yelled at to feel so loved and cherished by Ollie. Not that he didn't do that all the time; Ollie was constantly telling her she was beautiful (though Kerry couldn't exactly see how he made that one out) and making her feel special. She was so lucky...

Just like those two there, she smiled to herself as her gaze fell on a couple cuddled up together on one of the benches overlooking the river. The girl had her head on the boy's shoulder; the boy – *no, man,* Kerry corrected herself – had his arm draped around the girl's shoulders and was kissing her forehead.

A whine from Barney told her that his patience had run out and it was time to be on the move again.

"OK, Barney boy – I know," she smiled, bending down to pat the dog. "Pavements to pound, lamp-posts to sniff..."

Above the traffic's drone, Kerry's ears suddenly pricked up at the sound of distant laughter. She looked at Barney's ear, comically cocked in the air, as if he too had heard and recognised something in that sound.

Kerry turned and looked back over the bridge, joined by Barney, who'd stretched up on to his hinds legs – his forepaws on the stone parapet – to see what his mistress was looking at.

The laughter drifted over again as the girl tilted her head back at some unheard joke.

Barney, excited at spotting someone he knew very well, barked his hello.

"Barney!" hissed Kerry, ducking down behind the parapet and pulling the dog with her.

She was too shocked by what she'd seen – *who* she'd seen – to be aware of the curious glances of the passing motorists, all wondering what the girl with the dog was up to, bent double and tiptoeing her way along the pavement, like an extra in a spy movie.

CHAPTER 19

●●●●●●●●●●●●●●●●●●●●●●●●●●●●●

HIJACKING MAYA

Matt stretched his arms and gazed idly out of the plate-glass window.

"God, I'm knackered! Should've stayed in bed really; I'm only fit for Saturday morning telly..." he yawned. "That anniversary party I DJ'd at last night went on for ever and it was dead boring. Wasn't it, Joe?"

But Joe wasn't listening – he was staring at Kerry, who was nervously nibbling at the skin inside her lip and fidgeting with a silver ball of foil from her Kit-Kat.

"Joe?"

Matt looked from Joe to Kerry and then to the door, as Cat and Sonja sauntered into the café.

"Hurrah! The cavalry, come to save me!" he yelped.

"What are you on about?" asked Cat, sliding into the banquette next to Kerry.

"Well, these two here are about as entertaining as a weekend's worth of gardening programmes!" Matt moaned.

"Ah, give it a rest, Matt!" said Joe. "I'm tired too, y'know. And I'm sure I did most of the loading up of the gear at the end last night."

"Not true! I—"

But Sonja wasn't interested in what Matt was drivelling on about. She'd seen the strained look on Kerry's face and knew something was definitely wrong.

"Kez – what's up?"

"Uh, nothing!" said Kerry, with a startled look. "Maybe I'm just a bit tired today too..."

"Why? You were only babysitting Lewis with Ollie last night," Sonja pointed out.

"Ooh!" cackled Cat. "What were *you* two doing that's got you so tired this morning?!"

"Nothing! I didn't mean—" Kerry could feel herself blushing. Cat never missed a chance to tease someone with an innuendo and Kerry had walked right into that one.

"Tell 'em, Kez," said Ollie, coming over to the table and flopping a tea towel over his shoulder.

"Hee-hee, tell us what?" said Cat, raising her pencil-darkened eyebrows suggestively.

"Shut up, Cat," Ollie grinned at her. "Go on, Kez..."

"OK," shrugged Kerry. "It's just that I saw Maya last night and she was with someone."

Cat's eyebrows shot up so high they practically met her dyed blonde hairline.

"You mean like a *boy* someone? Wow!" she clapped her hands together excitedly as she gabbled. "So her tarot's coming true! So who is he? Who's the boy? Is it someone we know? Is it Billy?!"

"No," Kerry shook her head. "It's not Billy. And it's not exactly a boy either..."

Before a confused Cat could leap to any way-off-the-mark conclusions, Ollie stepped in and spilled the beans.

"It's Alex."

Cat's mouth was hanging open so wide that – if he hadn't been so surprised himself – Matt might have been tempted to throw Kerry's ball of Kit-Kat foil right into it.

● ● ●

"Here she comes!"

"Well, get away from the window then!"

Cat stepped back from Anna's front window, with its gauzy Indian fabric hangings, and stuck her tongue out at her cousin.

"Quick, everyone to their places!" ordered Sonja, pointing Kerry and Cat to the sofa.

"Take it easy, Son! We're not going to interrogate her," said Anna, motioning Sonja to calm down. "We're just going to have a nice chat, see what's going on, and if she's OK..."

Anna wasn't sure about this afternoon's hijacking of Maya, but the other girls had seemed so upset when they'd come clamouring at her door earlier, begging her to help them. And she hadn't been particularly keen on the idea of phoning Maya and asking her to come round and see her either. Maya had said "yes, of course" straightaway, but had sounded unsettled by Anna's unexplained request.

"Why can't you just talk to her about it when you see her in the café or something?" Anna had asked, when they'd first spelt out their plan.

"Because she might just deny it," Sonja had sighed. "I mean, think about the way that Alex bloke came charging into the Railway Tavern on Thursday night – something's obviously been going on for a while now and she's so uptight about it she's been keeping it secret from us!"

"Well, we don't *know* it's been going on for a while..." Kerry had interrupted.

"And *that's* what we need to find out. God, he could be pressurising her into this! He's a lot

154

older, isn't he?" Sonja flapped, full of concern for her friend. "Y'see, Anna, we need to confront her, but in a place away from distractions. That's why your flat's perfect. Our places are all full of annoying families who could interrupt!"

Anna had given in and given up her planned lazy Saturday off. Not that she minded; she cared about Maya's welfare – especially knowing what she did from their previous conversation in the flat – as much as the others did. It was only the subterfuge she found hard to deal with.

"I can hear her!" said Cat theatrically, inclining her head towards the door and the metallic clonk that was audible as Maya climbed the back stairs to Anna's flat.

Anna sighed, rolled her eyes and walked towards the doorway.

"Come on in, Maya," she smiled, ushering her friend inside.

"Hi! So what's–? Oh."

Maya stopped dead as she saw Sonja, Cat and Kerry staring back at her from Anna's small living room.

"Why do I feel like I've just walked into a courtroom?" she asked, glancing at each of her silent friends in turn.

"Maya," Anna smiled at her. "We're all a bit, well, freaked out."

"What about?" asked Maya, though she had a funny feeling she knew exactly what was on their minds.

"About you and... Alex," said Kerry, finding her voice. "I saw you two by the river last night, when I was out collecting Lewis."

Maya thought hard for a second. If Kerry had spotted them then there was no point denying anything. It was a pity. She and Alex had hoped to keep things quiet for a little while, till they were sure *themselves* what was going on.

"What's the deal with you and him then?" Cat blurted out in her usual blunt fashion. "Is he your boyfriend?"

"To be honest, I don't know," shrugged Maya. "But I know I'm happy."

There was a lot to be said, a lot to be explained, but it wasn't going to happen right at that second. The girls were so engrossed they hadn't heard the speedy steps clattering up the stairs, but they certainly heard the hammering knock on the door.

"Ollie!" said Anna in surprise. From what Sonja had said, all the boys were in on the plan for the girls to confront Maya – so why was Ollie interrupting?

"Sorry, sorry, sorry!" he said, bumbling into the living room, scraping the hair back from his face and looking slightly perplexed.

"What's wrong?" asked Kerry, getting up from the sofa and reaching towards him.

"It's OK, Kez," said Ollie, grabbing hold of her hand and sitting himself down on the arm of the nearest chair. "It's just... well, I needed a place to hide out for a bit."

"What?" squeaked Cat incredulously. "Who do you think you are, Ol? Some guy on the run from the Mafia?"

"I know it sounds stupid..."

Kerry watched as he talked. She could see the beads of perspiration glistening at the side of his face. Something had well and truly spooked him out.

"...but Nick left me alone to lock up downstairs in the caff and I was putting the dead bolt on the front door, when I saw someone staring at me from across in the launderette."

"What? Mad Vera?" asked Sonja, talking about the daft old dear who ran the place.

"No – *her*."

"Her who?" bleated Cat.

Ollie pulled a face as if to say, "You *know* who I mean – and I don't want to say her name out loud in case it's a jinx."

"What d'you mean? Stalker Girl?" said Sonja, finally clicking.

"Yeah, Astrid, or whatever she said her name was," Ollie shrugged.

Straightaway, Cat was on her feet, stomping over to the window for a bird's eye view of the launderette across the street.

"I know it sounds mad, but I didn't want to leave straightaway in case she came bowling over and made a scene," said Ollie, looking frazzled and embarrassed at the same time. "I just thought I'd come up and hang out with you lot for a while till she disappeared."

Kerry leant over and hugged him. So, her knight in shining armour needed help from the girlies after all...

"Can't see her," muttered Cat, staring out of the window like a net-twitching old granny. "But then I can't see all the way to the back."

"I'm going to stick some coffee on," said Anna, glad for Maya's sake that the change in topic had taken the heat out of the moment. The return of Stalker Girl wasn't exactly a bundle of laughs, but Anna was aware of the tension dropping away from Maya's shoulders.

"Sorry – did I, um, interrupt anything?" Ollie apologised with a hint of a knowing grin playing at the corners of his mouth.

Maya looked round at her friends. Kerry's big round eyes were like saucers; Sonja was staring intently; Cat's eyes were wicked and Anna's were smiling.

"You *could* say that!" Maya smirked as a ripple of laughter bubbled up in her chest. A split second later, all the girls – with Ollie looking bemused on his armchair perch – were all giggling till the tears streamed down their faces.

CHAPTER 20

● ●

HAPPYISH ENDINGS

"I think I'd better go and rescue Andy..."

"Why, what's up with him, Maya?" asked Joe, whose view of the bar was obscured by a newly arrived crowd of people.

"He's been surrounded by three girls who're flirting like mad with him – and he looks scared to death."

"How do you know they're flirting with him?" asked Joe, craning his neck to see what was going on.

"I've watched Cat in action often enough to spot serious flirting when I see it!" Maya smiled wryly, pushing her stool back and heading over to help Andy with the drinks and with his escape.

"Oi – I heard that!" Cat yelped after her, breaking away from her current conversation.

"You were meant to!" Maya laughed back over her shoulder.

"Right, anyway, *as* I was saying before I was so *rudely* interrupted," Cat continued, turning back to the others. "Tonight, we ask around and see if anyone knows who she is."

"Yeah, fair enough, Cat, but Stalker Girl might turn up herself anyway!" Billy pointed out.

"Astrid..." mumbled Ollie.

He felt she at least deserved the dignity of being called her real name. Even if she *was* bonkers and making his life a misery. Somehow, Ollie felt riddled with guilt over the whole situation. Maybe if he'd handled it better, or put her straight from the start, or been nicer to her the day she came into Slick Riffs, or been more *horrible* to her the day she came into Slick Riffs...

"I don't think she'll come tonight. Not after her yelling at Kerry last time we played here," Joe reasoned.

"But we said the same thing about her not turning up last week," said Sonja. "And *boy* were we wrong about that!"

"*And* you saw her spying on you from the launderette on Saturday," Anna chipped in.

Sitting with his friends and the band packed round a small table in the Railway Tavern, Ollie felt fidgety with all the attention. Having everyone focus on you when you were doing something fun like being on stage was one thing, but having them all analysing your life like this made him squirm.

"Well, maybe I got it wrong on Saturday – maybe it was someone who just looked a bit like her. I mean, you girls didn't see her in the launderette, did you? And I waited in your flat for ages."

"*And* ate all my chocolate Hob-nobs while you were at it..."

"Sorry, Anna," Ollie grinned. "I was tense – I needed to do something. I'll make it up to you – I'll buy you another packet, and a blueberry muffin, too, as interest!"

"Look, Ollie, we're trying to help you sort all this out," Cat interrupted sternly. Only it was hard to take seriously someone who was wearing a skin-tight T-shirt with the slogan 'Hi guys!' on it. "Do you want to stop making jokes for once and concentrate?"

"Sorry, Cat," Ollie apologised, pulling a pathetic face at her.

"So, you think we should ask people in the pub tonight if they know her?" Kerry asked.

"Yes," nodded Cat. "If we can find out what school or college she goes to or where she lives or works..."

"Well, what then?" Matt quizzed her.

Cat stared at him as if he'd asked the most ridiculous thing in the world.

"*I* don't know, do I? Hey, do I have to come up with *all* the ideas round here?" she said, holding her hands out in front of her pleadingly. "Isn't it enough that I come up with the *first* part of the plan?"

Sonja sighed and rolled her eyes to the paint-peeling ceiling. Cat could quite easily drive a person mad.

"I think this Astrid girl needs someone to have a quiet word in her ear," said Sonja. "And I don't mind being the person to do it."

"No, Son – if anyone speaks to her, it should be me," winced Ollie. Going through an awkward confrontation with Astrid came level with the idea of watching his Vespa go through a crusher in his personal list of nightmare scenarios, but if it came to the crunch, he knew he'd have to do it. For Kerry's sake if not for his own – he couldn't have people verbally abusing his girlfriend.

If only I hadn't been such a coward on Saturday, he told himself off. *If only I'd just stomped over to the launderette there and then and confronted her. Instead of running up the back stairs and hiding at Anna's...*

"What's the point in that, Ol?" said Sonja.

"If you talked to the girl, she'd either burst into tears or throw a garland round your neck and try to snog your face off!"

"This sounds interesting! Who's trying to snog whose face off?" asked Nick, catching the last of the conversation as he pulled out a spare stool and settled himself down with a slosh of his pint glass on the table.

"Stalker Girl. We're just taking bets on whether she'll turn up tonight and what surprises she'll pull if she does," shrugged Matt.

"Oh, *her*," Nick grimaced. Ollie had been keeping him up to date with the goings-on of The Loud's first officially overenthusiastic fan. "Well, you better get used to it, boys – if you hit the big time, you'll have more groupies than you'll know what to do with, and plenty of them will be as barking as her! Actually, I remember when I was on the road one time with Aerosmith, there was this girl who—"

While the others got ready to smile politely and laugh in the right places at the rock'n'roll anecdote Nick was about to tell – for the hundredth time – Cat turned her attention elsewhere.

"Yoo-hoo! Derek!" she called out to the pub's owner, who was clearing glasses from a nearby table. "Got a minute?"

Nick halted his story as he watched Cat wobble her way over to Derek in her high-heeled boots.

"What's she up to then?" he asked, scratching his stubbly chin.

"I dread to think!" said Sonja, noting the way her cousin struck several wiggly, coquettish poses as she chatted to the middle-aged man. It always amazed Sonja, the way Cat could stand up straight like a normal person when she was in the company of females, but automatically turn into an eyelash-fluttering contortionist in front of blokes.

Cat suddenly turned beaming towards them, with one thumb aloft, then reached for Derek's hand and dragged him over to their table.

"All right, Derek?" Nick nodded at him. "Cat been pestering you, has she?"

"Me, no!" Cat protested. "I've been playing detective, haven't I?!"

"What are you on about, Cat?" asked Sonja.

"Well, who would know the customers in here better than anyone? The person who runs it!"

"Ah!" said Matt, catching her drift. "So Derek, do you know this Stalk—"

Cat's eyes instantly widened at him, giving him an obvious red light on what he was about to say.

"Um..." he tried to backtrack, "...this girl who's been hanging round the band?"

"Astrid? I certainly *do* know her," nodded Derek. "She's my daughter."

There was a faint 'clink!' as Billy's glass collided with his teeth, but other than that, not a peep came from anyone seated around the table.

"Your friend here..."

"Cat," she simpered at Derek.

"Cat was saying our Astrid's been up to her old tricks. Been pestering you a bit, has she, Ollie lad?"

Ollie gave a nervous half-nod. It *sounded* like Derek was being sympathetic, but he didn't want to jump to conclusions. He didn't really want an irate dad knocking his teeth out and tearing up his band's Thursday night gig agreement.

"Don't worry, lad – she does this with every new band on the go around town," he shrugged. "Gets a bee in her bonnet about them, starts trailing them around, then takes it too far and makes a fool of herself. Me and her mum have told her time and time again, but... We just keep hoping she'll grow out of it."

"Uh... right," muttered Ollie, not sure what else to say.

"She's your *daughter*? Since when?" Nick exclaimed. "Last time I saw you and Eva with your kids they were two little things about *this* size, with pigtails and braces!"

"Hey, you know what teenagers are like, Nick,"

shrugged Derek. "Can't stand being around their folks, unless it suits them. That's what it's been like with Astrid anyway – never see her round this place unless there's a band playing. Thank God for our other daughter, Sacha – mind you, she's about to turn thirteen and she's getting into music too."

"Uh-oh," muttered Matt under his breath to Ollie. "Stalker Girl 2 – the sequel."

Ollie gave a cough, to cover up his sniggers.

"But don't worry, Ollie," said Derek, turning his attention back to his daughter's object of adoration, "I'll have a word with her about it. And anyway, she's probably bored with you by now. She's like that – two, three months following one band and she's off trailing another one."

"Well, you guys," said Matt, looking round at Billy, Ollie and Joe as soon as Derek had ambled off, empty glasses in hand. "So much for the loyalty of your first proper fan!"

"Can't say I'm going to lose sleep over it!" Ollie grinned, feeling his body go weak with relief. No confrontations, no more hassles for Kerry, no more staring out in the audience for a glint of diamanté and a pair of eerie staring eyes...

"What have I missed?" asked Andy, finally arriving back at the table with a trayful of glasses and bottles.

"The boys'll fill you in later – c'mon, take your drinks and get backstage," Nick ordered them jovially as he checked his watch.

"Where's Maya? I thought she was helping you, Andy?" asked Kerry as the boys all shuffled to their feet.

"Oh, she's talking to Alex – he's just arrived," he replied.

"Wow – he's come to see us again? He must really like our stuff!" grinned Billy, chuffed at his tutor's enthusiasm.

"Doh – I don't think he's come to see *you*!" Cat joked tactlessly.

Billy looked quizzically at Cat and then noticed the other lads had all headed off without him.

"Did you hear what Cat said just then?" he asked Joe, catching him up at the door to the corridor.

"Um, yeah," nodded Joe.

"Do you know what she meant?"

Joe hesitated before he replied: he knew Billy had had a thing for Maya way back last summer, and he was pretty sure that was all in the past. But it might be weird for him to hear that she and Alex were together. It had been weird enough for Joe to take in, but it wasn't as if he had a connection with Alex like Andy and Billy had – and neither of them had heard this little bit of news yet.

"Uh, Billy – Maya and Alex are... kind of seeing each other."

Billy stopped dead in his tracks in the scruffy corridor. Up ahead, the door to the dressing room banged shut as the others filed in.

"Since when?"

Uh-oh, thought Joe, seeing a tell-tale gutted look cross Billy's face. Joe knew what that felt like all too well.

"Since last week, I think. I don't really know exactly – I heard it second-hand from the others."

Billy stared down at the lino as if he'd find some explanation for all this scrawled down there.

"You want to hear something crazy, Joe?" he said, scuffing the toe of his trainer on the floor.

"What's that?" asked Joe.

"That fortune-telling stuff? That reading she got about finding true love? I kind of thought it was meant to be me..."

Seeing Billy's misery, Joe was half-tempted to spill everything out – tell him all about Kerry, all about the time he wasted, making himself miserable holding out for a girl he could never have. About how all the love songs in their set were written by him, and not Ollie, like everyone thought, and that every one of them was about Kerry – and no one knew *that*.

"Still," said Billy suddenly, raising his face

upwards and slapping a broad smile on it. "Plenty more fish in the sea, aren't there? Or at least plenty more gorgeous girls in the Railway Tavern tonight who might fancy going out with a guitarist in a top band!"

"Oh, yeah?" grinned Joe, who knew a brave face when he spotted one. "Is there a guitarist in a top band in here tonight?"

Joe ducked the jokey punch coming in his direction and both lads hightailed it, laughing, towards the dressing room door.

• • •

As the boys came on stage, Maya spotted Cat turn round and stare in her direction.

She'd give anything to come scurrying over here and give Alex the third degree, she smiled to herself, knowing that the other girls wouldn't let her.

Sonja, Anna and Kerry were giving Maya a little space and she appreciated it. She knew they still felt a little strange about what was going on with her and Alex, but they were trying to understand.

She'd take him over to join them in a little while, after she'd had him to herself a few minutes more.

"Happy?" Alex smiled down at her as they leaned back against the bar together.

Happy? Maya thought to herself. *What about scared and confused and uncertain and nervous...?*

But what was the point of worrying about the rest of it right now? She'd have to deal with it soon enough.

Maya rested her head against Alex's shoulder and sighed contentedly. "*Very* happy," she smiled back up at him.

Sugar
SECRETS...

...& Guilt

"So, what did she say to you?" Kerry asked Cat, at the same time wondering what was keeping Sonja this Saturday lunchtime. Kerry needed Sonja to be here, finding out what was going on in her cousin Cat's life, because Sonja would know what to do and say, unlike the boys, who were just making useless, sympathetic noises.

It's just like when we found out about Maya and Alex going out together, thought Kerry, glancing over the Formica table at Joe Gladwin and Matt Ryan. *None of us – not even Ollie – really knows what to say in the face of a big, scary, important situation.*

And to Kerry, Cat's situation did indeed seem big, scary and very, very important. The idea of being forced to move away from home, from your normal life, was just about Kerry's worst nightmare. (Not that she'd ever told anyone in case they said she was just being silly.)

Kerry glanced quickly at her watch – her lunch hour from the chemist's shop where she worked on Saturdays would be over soon and she'd have to run to make it back to the high street on time, but she just *had* to hear more of Cat's tale of woe.

"Well, Mum didn't say anything last night 'cause she switched off the TV and went to bed after that, and I didn't want to let on I was home."

"Why not, Cat?" asked Joe, looking confused.

But then, Cat confused him on a regular basis.

"Because I didn't want her to know I'd been listening in," she explained. Joe still looked puzzled.

"But did she speak to you this morning?" Kerry persisted.

"Oh, yes, she certainly did," replied Cat, rolling her eyes and folding her arms across her chest.

"*And?*" Matt chipped in, trying to hurry Cat along to the crux of the matter and not drag out the drama, which she was perfectly capable of doing.

"And she came out with all this stuff about taking a few days' holiday at short notice; how she's going off to the coast or somewhere tomorrow, with a pal of hers from the tennis club or something."

"But what did she say when you confronted her with the business about moving?" asked Kerry, her brow furrowing with worry.

"I didn't."

Matt and Joe both gave Cat an incredulous look.

"What d'you mean, you didn't?" asked Matt.

"Well, it's all about getting the upper hand, isn't it?" Cat pouted. "Like not letting her know I heard her on the phone: if she wants to keep this a secret from me, then *she'll* just look more of an idiot in the end."

"But, Cat, it's not about point-scoring, is it?" Kerry pointed out, trying to think what Sonja or Maya would say if they were here. "It's about finding out what's going on..."

"What's going on is that my mother either expects me to drop my friends and career prospects and trot off after her to God knows where," Cat shrugged huffily, "or she's thinking of deserting me."

"Cat, she wouldn't just up and leave you!" said Joe.

"Why not? My dad did!"

"Don't be so melodramatic!" Matt chided her.

"It's true!" Cat railed at him. "And who are you to talk, when your mother isn't exactly on the scene!"

"Cat, it's not that simple!" he argued, but deep down, Matt wondered why he was bothering. Maybe his mum hadn't just headed out the door one day and vanished into thin air like Cat's dad had done, but for all the effort she made to have a proper relationship with her son these days, the difference wasn't particularly noticeable.

"But either way, Cat, you must be freaking out!" said Kerry, her heart swamped with sympathy for her friend.

"Well, it's not like I get on with the old witch," said Cat, gazing soulfully out of the window of the End-of-the-Line café, "but what am I supposed to do if she *does* want to sell up and go on her own?"

"You'll *love* it, that's what you'll do," Matt grinned. "Independence at last. No more Sylvia sniping at you about being a disappointment of a daughter because of your college choice, or the colour of your hair, or the fact that the way you dress embarrasses her stylish sensibilities or whatever."

Cat flipped her gaze round to him, her whole face suddenly lit up.

"You know, it's not often I agree with anything you say, Matt Ryan, but just this once, you have a point!" she grinned back, her red-painted lips stretched into a bright smile. "This could be a whole new phase for me – making my way on my own, just like Anna..."

"Except Anna's got a job with a flat thrown in," Joe couldn't help pointing out.

"Maybe I should go and see one of the college advisers tomorrow – find out if there's any student accommodation going..." said Cat dreamily, ignoring Joe's comment.

"Might be difficult to find anything half-way through a term, Cat," Kerry pointed out gently. "And it's not like you even know *when* you might need to move in..."

"Maybe you could move in with Sonja – her old room's been empty since her brother moved out and she moved into *his* bedroom."

Kerry knew Matt was only stirring, but Cat didn't.

"What a brilliant idea! I'm sure Uncle Tom and Auntie Helena wouldn't mind. They've always said I'm like another daughter to them..."

"Uh, Cat," said Kerry warily, knowing exactly what *Sonja's* reaction to this conversation would be. "I think you should maybe hang fire with all these plans until you find out what exactly's going on from your mum. I mean, maybe she'll want *you* to stay in your flat!"

"Yeah, and *that's* likely," said Matt sarcastically. "Your mum's done pretty nicely out of her job and all, but it's not as if she's got a wodge of spare cash that she can afford to have *two* mortgages on the go."

"What, not like your big bucks dad, you mean?" Cat snapped. "Trying to rub our noses in how much *you're* worth again, rich boy?"

Matt hadn't meant to wind her up quite so much; he genuinely saw that it was potentially a weird time for Cat, but old habits – like teasing her to bits – died hard.

"C'mon, Cat," he smiled at her cheekily, trying to diffuse the situation. "You can always come and stay with me and my dad in our house – we've got too many rooms sitting doing nothing as it is."

"Really?"

Despite the fact that she was seventeen years old, wore more make-up than every girl in the End put together, and had a dirty cackle that would put Barbara Windsor to shame, at Matt's offer, Cat looked as sweet and trusting as a four-year-old.

"Yeah, of course," Matt nodded. "You could have the attic room. And the terms and conditions would be very attractive – free board and lodging, and all you'd have to do in return is wash our smelly socks and have a meal on the table every night!"

"Get lost!" said Cat, sticking her tongue out and no longer looking child-like as she realised her so-called mate was taking the mick. "I'd rather live with my mother till I'm eighty-five than come anywhere near you!"

A figure appeared at their table, shuffling from side to side and wringing a tea towel agitatedly.

"Sorry to interrupt, guys," said Nick Stanton.

"No problemo, Nick," said Matt, wondering why the café owner looked so stressed. Normally, he was totally laid-back, scratching his chin stubble, patting his beer belly and waffling on about the three most important things in his life: music, music and music.

"It's just that, well, Joe – I just wondered if you were free to help out here over the weekend, like you have before?" said Nick. "Anna's down with some stomach bug, and with it being food and everything down here, I don't really want her rushing back till she's properly better."

"Yeah?" replied Joe, concerned for Anna's welfare. "Hey, Nick, I *would* help out, but I'm off to the bus station in a minute. I'm going to my dad's for the weekend."

"Whoah!" interrupted Matt, glowering at Joe.

"Whoah, what?" asked Joe.

"Joey, mate, aren't you forgetting something?" said Matt, in his irritation forgetting something himself – the fact that Joe hated his name being lumbered with an additional 'y'.

"Like what?" asked Joe, frowning.

"Like you're meant to be helping me out tonight, at that anniversary party I'm DJing at?!"

"*What* anniversary party?"

"The one at the Balinard Hotel!"

"Well, maybe if you'd ever *mentioned* it to me, I might have kept this weekend free!"

Kerry, Cat and Nick watched as the conversation between the two lads batted back and forth. Ollie Stanton, wiping his hands as he sauntered over from his stint in the kitchen, caught most of it too.

"What?! I *told* you about it... *ages* ago!" said Matt indignantly.

"Like when?" countered Joe.

"Like... I can't remember!"

"Like you never asked!" Joe responded, looking as irked as mild-mannered Joe ever could.

"You know *your* trouble, Matt," said Catrina, pointing a long, painted nail at her friend. "You're so self-centred that you just supposed poor Joe here doesn't have a life. You thought all you had to do was whistle and he'd come running!"

Matt's face was slightly flushed with indignation. But then it never took much to stir up a battle of barbed words between him and Cat.

"I do not think that! I"

"And, let's face it," continued Cat merrily, "you haven't had a brain since Gaby chucked you. I mean, I know you've *said* you're over her, but you spend half your time in a daze. I bet you *didn't* ask Joe. I bet you"

"Hold up! Quit right there!" Ollie refereed, seeing by the hurt in Matt's face that Cat had hit a raw nerve. It was true, Ollie knew; Matt was finding it harder to get over Gaby than he'd thought...

ARE YOU A BOTTLER OR A BLABBER?

• •

Matt's dredged up some bad memories from the past, Maya's trying to make the best of a bad situation, and Cat – well, Cat's having a bad time all round. They're all dealing with it in different ways, but what would you do? Try our quiz and find out...

(1) There's major hassle in your life – what's your first reaction?

a) To lock yourself away in your room and slip into a pit of gloom.

b) To mull everything over till you can start making sense of it.

c) To pour your heart out to all your friends straight away.

(2) Your new boyfriend's great, but you know for sure that your parents won't approve. What do you tell them about him?

a) Nothing – even though it's going to be horribly complicated and a real strain trying to keep him a secret.

b) The bits you think they'll want to hear. You'll tell them more once they get used to the idea – and him.

c) Everything, all at once. And if they don't like it, that's *their* problem.

(3) You catch the end of someone's phone call, and you're sure they're saying something dodgy about you. Do you:

a) Say nothing, hope you're mistaken, but still worry yourself sick about what it might be?

b) Talk to the person later, giving them the opportunity to explain what's going on?

c) Ask them straight out what the hell they're playing at?

(4) Your kid sister gets away with anything at home. You:

a) Think it's hideously unfair, and silently resent her *and* your parents for giving in to her all the time.

b) Think it's deeply irritating but put up with it, since complaining to your parents makes you seem as childish as she is.

c) Throw a total strop next time it looks like she's going to get her way *again*.

(5) You're out one night, and you know you're showing off, but you're having too much fun to care. Then you overhear someone make a really bitchy comment about you. You're hurt. You'd tell:

a) No one in case they said, "Serves you right!"

b) Your best mate, 'cause she'll always be on your side, whatever.

c) All your mates, 'cause you'd want every bit of sympathy you can get.

6 You feel like your parents are neglecting you. Do you say something to them?

a) No – you'd feel like a baby. After all, you should manage to deal with things on your own at your age.

b) Only if the moment was right. You wouldn't want to blurt it all out when they weren't paying attention.

c) Too right – you'd make a real fuss if you thought they weren't being fair to you.

7 A friend asks if you're OK when you're feeling really lousy. Here's your chance to get things off your chest. Do you?

a) Probably not. You'd rather keep your worries to yourself than have people feel sorry for you.

b) Maybe – if you thought they could give you advice and weren't the type to go blabbing your problems to everyone.

c) Yes; you've been waiting for someone – anyone – to open up to.

8 Old photos, old love letters, old diaries. Do you look at them often?

a) No – they can bring back a lot of bad memories as well as good. It's better to forget about them.

b) Sometimes – it's weird to look back but it can be fun.

c) All the time. Why should you forget or hide the past?

(9) It's the perfect opportunity: there's only you and the person you most want to talk to in the room. Do you:

a) Chat about anything – except what's on your mind?
b) Take ages to work up the courage to say what you want to?
c) Blast them with everything that's been whizzing around your brain?

(10) Keeping a deep, dark secret to yourself makes you feel...

a) Miserable. But you'd be *more* miserable if everyone else knew about it too.
b) Very uncomfortable. You prefer everything to be upfront and honest.
c) Desperate to tell. You can't keep other people's secrets, and you struggle to keep your own.

NOW CHECK OUT HOW YOU SCORED...

SO, ARE YOU A BOTTLER OR A BLABBER?

• •

Mostly a

Bottle them up? You put your worries in a lead-lined safe and throw away the key! You think you're being very brave and adult by keeping problems and feelings to yourself, but all you're doing is making things twice as bad. Worries get magnified, small hassles become major nightmares, all because you're keeping them locked up inside. Find someone you trust, and tell 'em what's troubling you – honest, you'll feel a lot better for it.

Mostly b

You use your head, figuring out a lot of stuff on your own. But you know that keeping quiet when it comes to difficult situations is only a short-term solution; at some point you'll have to talk it out, because you're just not comfortable with keeping things bottled up.

Mostly c

Keeping things to yourself just isn't your style. Everyone knows everything about you, and if you've got something on your mind, they'll know about it sooner or later! Being straightforward is great, but only if you remember one important rule: think before you speak!

Coming in March 2000

Sugar
SECRETS...
...& Guilt

BOMBSHELL!
Eavesdropping leads to trouble for Maya...

SCARE!
And a big night out ends in anguish
for Cat.

GUILT!
Matt's haunted by the past; will his
recklessness spell disaster for them all?

*Some secrets are just too good to
keep to yourself!*

Collins
An Imprint of HarperCollinsPublishers
www.fireandwater.com

Coming in May 2000

Sugar
SECRETS...

...& Love

COLD FEET!
They say love never runs smoothly: Matt,
Anna and Maya would all agree with that!

SECRETS!
Ollie's hiding something – but what's it
got to do with Sonja?

LOVE!
Is all you need? Joe wonders if he'll ever
find that special someone...

*Some secrets are just too good to
keep to yourself!*

Collins
An Imprint of HarperCollinsPublishers
www.fireandwater.com

Sugar
SECRETS...
...& Revenge

LOVE!
Cat's in love with the oh-so-gorgeous
Matt and don't her friends know it.

HUMILIATION!
Then he's caught snogging Someone
Else at Ollie's party.

REVENGE!
Watch out Matt – Cat's claws are out...

Meet the whole crowd in the first ever
episode of Sugar Secrets.

*Some secrets are just too good to
keep to yourself!*

Collins
An Imprint of HarperCollins*Publishers*
www.fireandwater.com

Sugar
SECRETS...
...& Rivals

FRIENDS!
Kerry can count on Sonja – they've been best friends forever.

BETRAYAL!
Then Ollie's sister turns up and things just aren't the same.

RIVALS!
How can Kerry possibly hope to compete with the glamorous Natasha?

Some secrets are just too good to keep to yourself!

Collins
An Imprint of HarperCollinsPublishers
www.fireandwater.com

Order Form

To order direct from the publishers, just make a list of the titles you want and fill in the form below:

Name ....

Address ....

....

....

Send to: Dept 6, HarperCollins Publishers Ltd, Westerhill Road, Bishopbriggs, Glasgow G64 2QT.

Please enclose a cheque or postal order to the value of the cover price, plus:

UK & BFPO: Add £1.00 for the first book, and 25p per copy for each additional book ordered.

Overseas and Eire: Add £2.95 service charge. Books will be sent by surface mail but quotes for airmail despatch will be given on request.

A 24-hour telephone ordering service is available to Visa and Access card holders: 0141- 772 2281

Collins
An *Imprint* of HarperCollins*Publishers*